A SUMMER MCCLOUD PARANORMAL MYSTERY

FINLAY'S
FOLLY

a ghost story

NIKKI BROADWELL

AIRMID PUBLISHING
TUCSON, ARIZONA

Finlay's Folly

Cover design & formatting by Perry Elisabeth Design

ISBN-10: 0-9979941-5-0
ISBN-13: 978-0-9979941-5-5

DEDICATION

To my ever-patient husband, Jim, who has read and reread until his eyes crossed. I appreciate it more than I can say.

"Now I know what a ghost is. Unfinished business, that's what."
— Salman Rushdie, The Satanic Verses

CHAPTER ONE

I let out a yelp of surprise, turning to Jerry who had just placed his hands on my shoulders. "You scared me!" My attention had been focused on the sycamore trees, the dusky evening light limning the edges of their pale mottled trunks—sentinels in a protective line along the edge of my property.

"Where were you?" Jerry asked coming to stand beside me at the mullioned window.

"I was thinking about the cottage and the trees." My cottage had originally been the carriage house for the turn-of-the -century mansion behind. Mom had purchased the building back in the fifties and remodeled extensively, making it into what it was now—two bedrooms, one bath, a well-equipped kitchen and a living room with a fireplace. A large yard had been fenced along the side and back where ancient cherry and apple trees still produced fruit, despite the lack of care I gave them. In the spring daffodils would lift their yellow heads from the beds in front of the house, narcissus even earlier than that. The mansion behind now belonged to jet setters whom I rarely saw.

I turned to meet Jerry's brown eyes that looked soft in the gray light shining in. His half Italian heritage got me every time, the 'bedroom eyes' that soulfully stared into mine.

"I took off my shoes like you asked, and the rug must have muffled my steps," he apologized. "But you seemed pretty far away."

"The leaves are already falling," I complained, not sure why it bothered me so much. "It seems like yesterday we were at Agnes and Sam's wedding. Time seems to go by so fast."

It had been a whirlwind spring and summer with Agnes and Sam's wedding, and a school shooting that almost brought a halt to their plans. My occult shop, Tarot and Tea, had been torched during this same period of time, the act of violence related to all the rumors about devil worshippers that abounded as a result of the shooting; the incident had definitely brought the crazies out of the woodwork. Armed vigilantes had combed the forests, searching for the person or persons responsible, an innocent homeless man shot dead in the process.

The people who targeted my store were wound up from the newspaper articles that pointed to the occult as the perpetrators. The repairs had taken a lot of money and time. Thank goodness for the insurance policy my mother had taken out years ago.

"It is October, Summer. The leaves drop at this time of year. We could celebrate the changing season in the bedroom." His eyebrows rose suggestively before he lifted my chestnut hair and kissed the back of my neck, sending little shivers down my spine.

I pulled away. "You are incorrigible! I thought you

had some paperwork to finish up before dinner."

He shrugged, a frown appearing between his dark brows. "It can wait. I told you the current chief is leaving and Sam won't be back from the honeymoon for another week. I'm doing double duty these days." He grinned. "That's why I need some down time. What do you say?"

"So you won't be chief?"

Jerry shook his head. "I don't want to be chief. It's a thankless and stressful job. I like being a detective. Sam and I make a good team."

I made a moue. "You and Sam…what about me?"

Jerry smiled. "Thought that would get you going. Yes, my little amateur sleuth—you're the best."

"You'd *better* say that after all we've been through." Our last case, or *Jerry's* last case—the shooting—had included a ghost from the past, who appeared to me with hints. In the meantime the chief had railroaded a woman who I was sure was innocent. But when everything was said and done, Sarah had disappeared with her half-brother, leaving the entire police force wondering—could Harry Dreiser have done it? Normally Jerry would have been like a hound on a scent, but for some reason he had never followed up, chalking the entire situation up to ghosts and weirdness. "So who do you think will get the thankless job?"

Jerry's gaze slid away. "Myra is filling in until some candidates can be vetted."

I thought of beautiful Myra, the DA, a woman on the list of Jerry's past girlfriends. "Hmm…that should be interesting." But before I could go further along this train of thought, he grabbed my hand and dragged me into the bedroom. "Shoo," I heard him say, watching my two cats, Mischief and Tabby, flee out the door. Cutty, my part Jack Russell terrier, gave a bark of protest when Jerry pulled the door closed in his face. I was about to protest when Jerry took my face in his hands, his mouth meeting mine.

"Be here now, Summer," he murmured, unbuttoning my shirt. He pulled it open, his warm hands moving across my skin. And then he kissed me.

CHAPTER TWO

Jerry left early the next morning, leaving me with two disgruntled cats and an annoyed dog. Dinner for us had never materialized. The talking and 'other activities' had given me a more secure feeling about Jerry being around Myra Proctor every day. But I had to admit I did feel some trepidation, especially if she was up for anything. He had a hard time saying no, especially to beautiful women.

I took a shower and dressed in a long skirt, leather boots, and a hip length sweater. I had to start looking a bit more professional in my role as owner of Tarot and Tea. And the fall weather rendered my bare feet, peasant blouses and long gypsy skirts inappropriate. I checked the temperature outside before pulling on my heavy cabled sweater coat: 35*. "Be good," I told Cutty as I closed the front door. He stared at me, an unhappy expression on his whiskery face.

Even my Honda junker seemed to be watching me with a scowl as I headed toward it. "Don't tell me you're annoyed too," I said quietly, climbing in. "Sorry about your bald tires and your dirty oil, but I don't have the money right now." I turned the key and brought the engine into what life it had. I patted the dashboard.

"You're a keeper," I said, trying not to worry about the little hiccups I heard. After all, it was a cold morning. I backed out and pulled away from the cottage.

Even though it was only a couple of miles from my house to Tarot and Tea, it was nice to have some heat along the way. I grabbed the leather gloves with the rabbit fur lining out of the glove compartment and pulled them on. The steering wheel was ice cold.

I was driving slowly, allowing the engine to warm up before I shifted into second gear, when a loud horn blared behind me. I pulled over, letting an impatient man in an SUV tear by. "Learn how to drive!" he yelled out his open window, his middle finger held up. Was it the 'holidays', soon to be upon us, that made people so ill tempered?

When I opened the door to Tarot and Tea I could still smell the fresh varnish from my new shelving, the tang of floor cleaner on the hickory flooring. I felt pleased with the gleaming shelves, the handsome dark boards under my feet. They were veneer, but who would know? When I thought of the person or persons responsible for the fire I turned my thoughts elsewhere. They had never been apprehended, but I no longer worried that it was someone who lived in Ames. At least I hoped not.

"My dear! I wondered if you would make it on time this morning!" I looked up from opening the register to see Mrs. Browning entering the shop.

"Why wouldn't I?" I asked, peering at her. She looked perky this morning, dressed in a long wool skirt and bright sweater, a black beret on an angle to cover her gray hair. She was a fixture here, and I still had not been able to determine if she were a ghost or not. I tended to think yes, but without asking her directly I might never know for sure.

"I thought you mentioned that you and your handsome policeman had some catching up to do—you know." She waved her hand in the air.

What? I was sure I had said no such thing. But it *was* Monday morning. Perhaps she thought we'd had a big weekend or something.

"Is your sweetheart planning to propose anytime soon?"

I opened my mouth and closed it. "Um…we aren't anywhere near marriage, Mrs. Browning."

"Oh, you young people and how you view life. In my age a girl would never shack up with a man before marriage. Not that I'm chastising you, dear. Your free-spirited mother was just the same."

I found myself smiling despite my irritation. My mother had never married any of the men she lived with, including my father. Free spirit hardly did her justice. "Marriage doesn't mean as much as it used to. It scares people because they worry about being trapped."

"So silly, really. A man can be such a comfort and a protector, not to mention a provider."

I turned back to the register. "Most women support themselves now. And a lot of women don't want to be protected."

I heard her scoff of disapproval as she headed into

the stacks where the goddess books lived.

My cell phone rang around noon, Jerry's name on the screen. I slid my finger across. "What's up?"

I heard his chuckle before he said, "Wouldn't you like to know."

"Jerry, I don't have time for this banter," I whispered. "I have customers."

There was a slight pause. "Just wanted to tell you that Myra's stint here will probably be shorter than I thought. Apparently there are several well-qualified candidates up for chief, and the council will be deciding as soon as next week."

"That's good, I guess. How's it going with her there?"

"Just about how you imagined it would be. She's poised and competent and fair."

And sexy, with long legs and big eyes. "Glad to hear it. Is that the only reason you called?" I asked, noticing Douglas approaching the register.

"Pretty much...I was thinking about us, and...crap...I have to go."

I placed the phone on the counter, my attention on Agnes's father. I liked Douglas very much, with his white hair, and tweed suits and vests from a bygone era. Despite being a ghost, or maybe because of it, he always looked impeccable.

He gave me a penetrating stare. "Is he about to

16

propose?"

How did he know who I was talking to? "What is going on today—first Mrs. Browning and now you? Why does everyone think Jerry is about to ask me to marry him?"

He raised his eyebrows, a smile lightening his features. "After Agnes it could be catching, you know."

I shook my head, frowning. "Hardly. Jerry and I...we seem to get close for a while and then we break up, and then..."

"Get close once again...I've been there, Summer."

I knew the long history of Agnes's mother, Serena, and Douglas. They loved each other while Serena married other men, using her skills with poison to do them in. My mother had been Serena's best friend, and from what I'd gleaned since her death, she was involved with Serena in these endeavors, even referring to Serena as the 'black widow' in letters I'd discovered in a box of her papers. And when I read notes about these men, I figured they all deserved to die, especially since they were too wealthy to be touched by the police. But that was way before my time.

I shook my head to clear thoughts of Lila. She had appeared to me at the local coven, but I had the sense that she'd moved on now.

"Did you know the coven is no more?"

"Are you saying we won't have a meeting on the full moon?"

Douglas nodded, leaning in to whisper. "The rumors have been flying fast and furious, and because of it, the police will be staking out our spot by the river."

I swung my gaze toward him. "The police? Why would they care?" This couldn't be true. There were at least a hundred people in the coven now.

"The townsfolk have been talking about devil worshippers for months, making up stories about animal sacrifice and spells. The churchgoers have complained to the local constabulary. The coven will go underground, Summer. Mark my words."

I'd missed several full moon ceremonies due to the wedding and my duties as wedding planner. "Will you please alert me when they do?"

Douglas nodded, handing over his little bottle of rosemary oil. "Helps with memory," he explained, holding out a twenty-dollar bill.

I nodded, distracted by his news. Once I'd given him his change he left the store, making sure to open the door and close it after him, even though he could have walked right through it.

When I closed up the store at five my mind was still puzzling over what Douglas had told me. Maybe the coven meetings could be held at the Victorian old age home that Agnes had so lovingly re-furbished with money she'd inherited from her mother. The ballrooms alone were certainly large enough. My mind turned to the rumors about witches, wondering who could be spreading them. I turned down the street toward the bakery. Becky would know.

The bell tinkled when I opened the door into the bakery, a miasma of mouth-watering smells wafting toward me. The stainless steel ovens were off now, pristine and sparkling where they waited for the next morning's loaves, scones and sticky buns. Becky was about to close up, doing some last minute cleaning before she left the shop. As soon as she turned from her sweeping I launched into my question.

"No one told you?" she asked. "I guess you've been so involved with getting your shop up and going again, and with the wedding, and…"

"And the shooting, and on and on," I finished for her. "But still…do you happen to know who told the police about our meetings?"

"I think this was largely due to the school shooting last spring. People went kind of crazy, and the town seemed to attract a bunch of nut-jobs from other places." She pushed wisps of strawberry blonde hair back behind her ears. Her face was flushed, the bakery still over warm from the ovens. "I'm sorry I didn't mention it."

"It's not your fault. I counted on the coven, since it's the only time I ever got to see Mom. Now I'll never see her, and I have no other relatives I can talk to. It makes me feel lonely."

Becky smiled. "You have another relative here."

I frowned. "Besides Mom? Who?"

Becky smiled. "The guy in the graveyard you told me about."

I stared at her. "That guy? I think it was a fluke that

he showed himself that night."

Becky pulled her apron off and hung it on a peg by the front door. "You told me you planned to go back and see him again. Have you?"

I thought about Finlay Ross McCloud who happened to be sitting on the edge of his gravestone when Jerry and I were grave robbing, trying to solve our last case. Besides Jerry, Becky was the only other person I'd confided in about him.

"When did you say he lived? The 1800's?" Becky asked.

"He died in 1884. But why should I talk to him?"

"You said you wanted a relative to talk to. He must know all kinds of things from way back when. Maybe the coven was going on and he was a member."

"Just because he's a ghost doesn't mean he's a witch."

"Warlock, Summer. Anyway, just a suggestion. From what you said, he sounded interesting."

I smiled, thinking of the dapper man wearing a vest under his long black coat, a tweed cap on his head. "He was interesting."

By the time I fed Cutty and the two cats it was nearly dark. I watched the color leach from the sky, my plans to take a walk to the graveyard fading along with the light. But when Jerry called to tell me he was heading to his mother's house, I knew he wouldn't be back for dinner.

His mother was a master manipulator and had no fondness for me—she tried to do subtle things to break us up whenever she had the chance. As I nibbled on a cracker I thought about Finlay Ross McCloud.

Five minutes later I was in my bedroom closet retrieving my down coat. Before heading out the front door I grabbed the leash and hooked it to Cutter's collar. A walk was just what I needed, and if by chance Finlay was feeling sociable—well, that would be okay too.

CHAPTER THREE

By the time I reached the graveyard I was seriously wondering about my sanity. With the clear sky it had turned windy and bitter cold, and I hadn't thought to wear gloves, my hands sunk deep into the pockets of my coat. I was already shivering as I pulled up the hood around my wind-burned face.

I entered the rocky uneven section of the graveyard through a small creaky gate, my gaze going to the ancient gnarled trees that looked like skeletons waving their arms in the breeze. The waxing moon was close to half full, the gravestones casting elongated shadows across the silvery ground. Limbs complained as they rubbed together, sending dry leaves swirling to the ground, where they moved and spun like something alive. Ghost-like shapes flitted here and there, shimmering for a moment before disappearing again.

Why had I decided to come here? But just as I turned to leave, Cutty gave a sharp bark and I saw my ghost. The lower half his body was in shadow, the upper half, bright in the moonlight. He looked corporeal where he sat on the edge of the gravestone, a smile of welcome on his face when he saw me. I moved toward him, stumbling on rocks and roots.

"Hello," I began, not knowing what to call him—Mr. McCloud? Finlay? The last time I'd seen him he hadn't said anything. Could he even speak?

That question was answered when I heard him say, "Hello, lass," in a deep brogue. "I hoped ye would return."

"Time means something to you?" I asked, moving closer. He was dressed as he had been the last time, his clothes varying shades of gray in the moonlight.

"Time is of no importance where I am. But seein' ye here before brought me into your world. I had something to say to ye that night, but you and your man got away before I had the chance."

I sat on the edge of the gravestone next to his, watching Cutty sniffing around his feet. My dog looked up at him and gave a little woof. "Cutty can see you? How is that possible?"

He shrugged. "Animals are far more sensitive to the departed than humans. Ye happen to be a special case, lass."

"Did you know we're related?" I asked him. "I'm a McCloud too."

"Aye. 'Tis why I wished to talk with ye. Judging by how I'm stuck here, it seems my death needs to be resolved before I can move on."

I stared, surprised. "I'm not a detective."

He chuckled. "I saw ye here that night diggin' up some old bones to solve yer case. I heard ye talkin' to yer copper. The two o' ye were in it up to yer eyeballs. 'Tis nae as though I can go to the local constabulary and ask them to solve it."

"For your information there weren't any bones in the casket. All we found were rocks."

He laughed. "'Tis naught to me, lass. I am merely pointin' out yer proclivities."

"But if you were murdered it was a long time ago. The person who did it is long dead."

He nodded, reaching down to rub Cutty's ears. His fingers went right through. Cutty wagged his tail. "It will be a merry chase for ye, to be sure. It all started back in the Highlands. 'Tis where ye'll need to begin."

"Scotland? Are you kidding? I have a business to run and no money for a trip."

"County Sutherland in the Highlands, to be exact," he continued, ignoring me. "Up in the northwestern corner. Canna rightly remember it now, but there's a castle, and…" He stopped and scratched his head. "Stones…built of gray stone, ye ken."

"If you were killed there, why are you here in Ames?"

He frowned, seeming confused. "The murder must have happened here. But whoever did it was from the old country."

"How do you know?"

"Must have been the manner of it. The only part I recall is that it came from behind," he said, his dark eyes puzzled.

"So you think maybe someone snuck up on you from behind and stabbed you. Is that it?"

He brightened, as though my words brought it all

back. "Now ye have it...a cowardly way to kill a man. Must have been a lad from the Highlands who had a bone to pick."

I laughed. "A bone to pick? Sounds a bit more than that. Who did you piss off?"

He stared at me, uncomprehending.

"Sorry—who did you anger enough to make them want to kill you?"

Finlay suddenly looked around, his eyes widening. "Must gae now. Make yer plans and we'll talk again." He disappeared, leaving me staring at his headstone. Cutty whined.

I clipped on the leash, my senses picking up some entity that I did not want to tangle with. There was a glow on the other side of the graveyard, and I noticed that any other ghosts who'd been hanging around had disappeared. I wondered if it could be the guy who killed Finlay. I shivered and hurried through the little gate and jogged toward home.

When I entered the cottage Jerry was in the kitchen with a beer in his hand. "Where have you been?"

His eyes were narrowed in anger, as though my absence was directly aimed at him. Were all men this self-centered? "I figured you'd be a while, Jerry. I took Cutty for a walk."

His eyes widened. "A walk? It's freezing out there!"

I shrugged and took off my coat, glad to see he'd made a fire. "How's your mother?"

He shook his head and stared at the floor. "As

annoying as ever. She's at me again about moving in." His gaze met mine. "She does seem frail."

I knew that look. "So you're considering it?"

"No. I'd go nuts if I had to live with her, but she needs someone to check on her. I'm afraid she'll fall or something."

"Help, I've fallen and I can't get up?" I quipped.

He smirked. "Something like that."

I moved to the fire and stood in front of the flames, glad for the warmth on my back. "I saw Finlay tonight."

"Finlay—who's that?"

"Remember my relative in the graveyard…the one who I think pushed me into the mud that night?"

Jerry chuckled and moved beside me to warm himself. "Finlay Ross McCloud," he said. "What is his relationship to you?"

"He could be my mom's great great grandfather. Is that far enough back for someone born in the eighteen hundreds?"

"I'd have to work it out on paper. What were you doing in the graveyard?"

I let out a sigh, wondering if I should tell him the entire story. "Becky mentioned him earlier today, and for some reason I was drawn there. He wants me to find the person who murdered him."

"What?" Jerry gaped at me.

"He said he couldn't move on until it's resolved."

Jerry scoffed and shook his head. "If he died that long ago there's no way to trace it down now."

"He told me he was stabbed in the back."

"That helps," he said sarcastically. "If he doesn't even know who did it, how can you figure it out? If I were you I'd go to the museum and see if there are any records on the dude."

"He thinks I need to go the Highlands of Scotland. I looked Sutherland up on Wikipedia and it's the northwestern most county on the mainland."

"What...why? He was killed here, Summer."

"He says that's where the story begins. It sounds like maybe the man who killed him has family there. Maybe he went back home after Finlay was dead. Finlay came from there too."

Jerry scoffed. "Go to the museum and see what they have to say. There's lots of records about the early days in Ames."

"I will, but if I don't find anything I may want to go to Scotland. The trip sounds fun."

Jerry frowned. "I can't go right now. There's too much happening at the station. Looks like the council won't decide on the new chief until after the New Year."

"I didn't ask you to go along, Jerry. The fact that I'm even thinking about is crazy, I know."

Jerry took a swig of his beer, choking. "You'd go to Scotland alone?"

"I...I don't know yet."

He shook his head. "It's a ridiculous idea, especially since the dude's been dead for over a hundred years. How could you possibly solve a case with so little to go on? What's got into you?"

I heard the implied 'without *me*, the hot detective, by

your side'. "I haven't made up my mind. First I'll check out our local museum. If I did decide to go, you'd have to look after the animals. And someone would have to take care of Tarot and Tea."

He banged his beer down on the table next to the couch and sat heavily. "Damn it, Summer. I was thinking that we—" But before he could finish his sentence, his cell phone rang and he stopped to answer it. He mumbled some words I couldn't hear and stood. A moment later he'd rung off. "Mom needs me." He reached for his leather motorcycle jacket and pulled it on.

"What happened?"

"She fell, and it sounds like she may have broken her wrist." He ignored the sound I made in the back of my throat as he picked up his keys and left the house. A moment later I heard his Indian motorcycle growl into life and then the roar as he took off down the street.

I went to the kitchen and poured myself a glass of wine, my mind spinning in a zillion directions. I'd just blurted out my entire conversation with Finlay, but I wasn't anywhere near making a decision. The idea of flying off to Europe to look for a ghost was insane. And if Finlay was killed here, why wasn't his murderer in the graveyard with him?

But underneath all these questions a little voice was egging me on. I glanced down at Cutty who sat staring at me with bright eyes. "What do you think, Cutty?" He wagged his tail and barked, but I couldn't interpret the message.

CHAPTER FOUR

Jerry did not come home that night, and although I knew I should probably be concerned about his mother, I wasn't. Instead, I felt annoyed that she'd managed to keep him at her house overnight. I thought of the mansion on the hill where she and her husband, the former chief of police, had made their home. They'd had a slew of servants back then. Why not now? Especially since Jerry's father was dead and she lived alone. Had the pension dried up due to Jerry's father's illegal activities? I had no sympathy for her.

When Jerry called the next morning it was close to nine. I was in the car on my way to Tarot and Tea.

"Did you miss me?"

"Oh, weren't you there last night?"

"Very funny. It took fucking forever to get out of the ER, and Mom was completely freaked out by the time we got home."

"I bet she was," I muttered.

"What's that?"

"Nothing. Was her wrist broken?"

"Worse than that...she had to have a cast above her elbow. And it's her right hand."

"She'll need help, won't she? What are you going to

do?"

"What do you think? I'm moving in with her until I can find proper help."

"What about one of your sisters—Eliza or Celeste?" Those were the only two of Jerry's many siblings I'd met. Somewhere he had two brothers stashed, but I had yet to meet them.

"They both have families and live too far away."

"And your brothers?"

"Stephen lives on the west coast and Michael lives in Florida. They're both lawyers, so I doubt they can drop everything and come up here to stay with Mom."

"Bet your mom is proud," I mumbled. "One police detective and two lawyers. Wow."

"Stop being snide, Summer. She really needs me right now."

I pulled the car up to the curb in front of Tarot and Tea and shut off the motor. "I'm sorry, but your mom is always doing stuff like this. And every time it happens, you jump in to help her and take yourself away from our relationship and me. Have you talked to her about selling the mansion and moving into assisted living?"

"Are you kidding? She'd never go for that. The house is everything to her."

"She needs full time help, it seems. What happened to the maids I saw scurrying around at your dad's wake? Did they all leave due to her nastiness? I really hate how you jump when she whistles."

He let out a heavy sigh. "She let the help go a while back, said it bothered her having them underfoot. She hates strangers being in her house."

"How long this time?"

"I hope it won't be more than a few days. I'll come by after work and pick up my things."

"I wish our relationship meant more to you," I grumbled.

"About that—I wanted to talk to you about something, but I guess it will have to wait."

"Yeah, especially with you living with your mom again."

When he disconnected I stuck the phone in my bag and hurried toward the store.

"On the phone again with that nice young policeman, dear?" Mrs. Browning asked when I walked past her to unlock the door.

"His mother broke her wrist," I answered, swinging the door open to let her inside. I reached around and flipped on the lights.

"She's not in favor of the marriage, is she?"

"What marriage?" I yelled. This was day two of innuendo. What did she know that I didn't?

"I'm sorry to upset you, Summer. I just thought he might have proposed."

"Well, he didn't. And if he had, I would've turned him down," I snapped, heading to my desk.

She gave me a concerned look before heading into the stacks again. I watched her pull out a book, peruse it and slip it back, only to take down another and thumb through the pages. The way my clients acted you'd think this was a library, not a place of business.

I pulled the loose receipts from the past month out of the drawer and began to organize them, placing them in the proper folders. Good thing I had the back-up system of the computer. I had to face the fact that the amount of money coming in would not keep this place going. I needed a new plan to get people buying instead of browsing. I sighed and bent to it, hoping sales would pick up. Having the store out of commission for several weeks had not helped.

I was hard at work when Becky came in, her face flushed, a butter and flour-stained apron over her sweater and jeans. "I brought you some breakfast since you skipped it this morning." She placed a cup of coffee with cream and a cheese croissant on my desk.

I smiled. Becky was a proper witch, her intuition always right on target. "I did skip it. I was distracted this morning."

"Jerry?" she asked mildly.

"Among other things." I watched Mrs. Browning hurrying toward the door without buying anything. I hoped shouting at her hadn't put her off. She was normally one of my best customers. "I took your advice and went to the graveyard last night," I whispered, looking around. There were only two other people in the store, and neither one seemed very interested in eavesdropping.

"And did you see him?"

I nodded. "He wants me to find out who murdered him."

Becky's green eyes grew round. "Someone in

Ames?"

"Years ago, yes. But he wants me to go to Scotland." I glanced around again before leaning forward. "He says that's where it all began."

"My family's from Scotland," Becky said. "Did he say where?"

"County Sutherland in the Highlands But I need to visit the local museum first and see if they have any records. After that I'll talk to him again. I don't have near enough to go on."

"My family's from around Inverness. Have you heard of Findhorn?"

"What's a findhorn?"

"It's an eco village or spiritual community close to Inverness. If you go you should definitely visit there."

I stared toward the door, watching bright leaves whirl by. The wind was picking up again. If this continued there wouldn't be a leaf left on any of the trees. "Jerry can't go with me."

"You'd be fine on your own. But if you're thinking about the next few months, the weather can be nasty. I'd say go now if you're going to do it."

"I have to say it sounds exciting. But I would need someone to watch the store. I was thinking Agnes, but by the time they get back from the honeymoon she'll be too close to her due date; she probably won't want to sit here and deal with customers. But I'm getting ahead of myself. First I need to check the death records at the Ames Museum."

"I can find someone to watch the store." She looked

at her watch, a frown appearing between her ruddy brows. "Gotta fly. We'll talk later."

I watched her run to the door and hurry through, her braids lifted by the wind. I imagined her riding a broomstick, the image not so far-fetched.

At lunchtime I put the shut sign on the door and climbed into my Honda. The museum wasn't far and I figured it would take less than an hour to find out what I needed.

"Records from a death in 1884?" The gray-haired woman pulled on the glasses hanging around her neck. "I'm only a volunteer here. I hope I can locate what you need." She clacked away on the computer for a few moments before looking up at me. "As far as I can tell there is no record of the death of a Finlay Ross McCloud in Ames in 1884. You could check on the microfiche at the library—they might have an old newspaper obituary."

"Thanks. I will." I left the museum and hurried to the library down the street.

"Oh no, dear. We don't do microfiche anymore. Check in there," she said, pointing toward a darkened room. "The birth and death records date back quite a ways. Check the spines for the year you're searching."

I headed toward where she pointed, turning on the light as I entered the room. I found a thick leather bound book and pulled it out, laying it open on the table. I thumbed through the alphabetized names under September of 1884, but there was no Finlay Ross McCloud listed. In fact there were no McClouds at all.

I stopped at the desk again, waiting until the woman

looked up from her work. "There's a headstone in the graveyard with the name Finley Ross McCloud, but there's no obituary."

"Not every death was written up in the paper, dear. One had to be important to have an obituary listed."

"Thanks," I said, disappointed that I hadn't discovered something more.

∞

It was close to five when the shop phone rang, startling me from where I was re-shelving the essential oils. My customers had left them scattered in an untidy mess. I backed down the ladder and hurried to my desk to pick up my cell. "Yes?" I asked, annoyed.

"Don't take your crap out on me, Summer. Just because I have a mother to deal with, doesn't mean--"

"That's uncalled for, Jerry."

"So why did you answer like I'm some pariah?"

"I didn't know it was you. I was on a ladder and...now that you brought it up, the idea of you moving out doesn't exactly make me happy. We just got a routine started and I like having your solid body next to mine in the bed."

Jerry chuckled. "Don't think I won't miss your sweet little body next to me. It doesn't mean I can't visit you, though."

I could almost see the suggestive waggle of his eyebrows, his meaning quite clear. "When is that going to happen? Won't Mummy need her Jerrykins?"

He let out an exasperated sigh. "I can't help what's going on. She needs me and I'm here. She is my mother, after all."

I let a moment tick by and then another, waiting for him to tell me why he called. "It's closing time now. I'm heading home," I finally said into the silence.

"I'll meet you there," he muttered before he hung up.

I closed up and drove slowly through town, concerned about the missing beats going on in my Honda's engine. It seemed I might need to take it in sooner rather than later. I didn't have the money right now. And then I thought about my proposed trip to Scotland, wondering what in the world I was thinking. After going through my latest receipts I was positive there was no extra money to be had. But since my visit to the museum, I had to say my interest was piqued. The lack of information on Finlay in the library and museum records, seemed to indicate a real mystery—and I did enjoy solving puzzles.

I held my breath when my car missed and nearly quit. The wind was blowing trash everywhere, people rushing off the sidewalks to avoid whatever horrible weather was coming in. From how cold it was I wouldn't be surprised if it snowed. I managed to make it home, pulling into the space next to Jerry's motorcycle.

"Hey!" I called out once I was in the living room. I heard the shower and headed into my bedroom where I slipped off my shoes and coat. I sat on the edge of the bed next to Cutty, listening to Jerry's baritone singing *oh sole mio* at the top of his lungs. At least he was in a good mood.

I was leaning against the headboard with my eyes closed when he emerged with a towel wrapped around his lower body. "Just the person I wanted to see," he said, dropping the towel and heading toward me.

I frowned, moving out of reach. "Not now, Jerry."

"Why not now? I can't stay long. I told Mom I was picking up a few things and would make her dinner when I got back."

"Sorry, but I'm not in the mood for a 'wham bam, thank you, ma'am'. I have a lot on my mind."

His lips pressed together in annoyance as he headed to the bureau. I watched him pull on a pair of plaid boxers and clean jeans. Once he had his shirt buttoned he added the gun holster he'd left on the side table. When he swiveled toward me I was not thrilled with the expression on his face.

"You know, Summer, you've really put me in a bad mood tonight. I'd hoped we could take some time for each other before I left. I had something I wanted to talk to you about, and I don't know when we'll get another chance."

"You said you'd visit."

He turned his back to get his keys and change off the dresser before he pulled open the drawers again and extracted more underwear, shirts and jeans. I watched him grab his duffel from the shelf in the closet and stuff things in. "Mom is insistent that I come home right after work. She says she's in pain and can barely reach up to get a glass off the shelf."

Come home? This was his home now. "Did my name come up during your discussions?"

"No, actually, it didn't."

"So, she either has no idea you're living with me, or she doesn't care?"

"She may not know. I haven't mentioned it."

"Oh great." I shook my head. "Did you say you wanted to talk to me about something?"

"Now is not the right time."

And before I could think of a retort he had crossed the living room and was opening the front door. "I'll come by and get my espresso machine during lunch tomorrow," he called out. I heard the door slam and a moment after that his motorcycle started up.

I sat on the couch trying to stop the sudden bout of tears that forced their way out of my eyes. The espresso machine was a symbol of us being together…and now he was taking it to his mom's house? I knew I'd been a brat about his mom, but this was too much. He hadn't even bothered to tell her we were together. I had a sinking feeling about our future. Cutty jumped on the couch as if to console me, snuggling close. He loved Jerry as much as I did, but I got the impression that in this case, he was on my side.

CHAPTER FIVE

I spent a restless night, my dreams full of ghosts who wanted things from me, and images of Jerry's mother staring at me with an expression of loathing. By the time I woke I was tangled up in the covers, my skin clammy.

As soon as I opened my eyes I knew that the predicted storm had arrived, wind screaming around my cottage, and the worrisome sounds of limbs hitting my roof. Cutty shivered next to me, his eyes wide with fear. "It'll be okay, little guy. These thunderstorms never last long." I rubbed his ears before I disentangled my legs and stumbled toward the bathroom to take a shower.

In the kitchen later I made what I figured was my last cappuccino for a while, at least one that wouldn't cost me anything. I drank it leaning against the counter, staring mindlessly out the window at the storm. Downed tree limbs littered my yard, and someone's trash had overturned, spreading empty food cans, plastic containers and paper everywhere.

Just as I was thinking the storm was moving past it began to snow. "Oh great," I muttered, realizing that not only was my car not working properly, but also the tires were nearly bald, and I had no chains. A moment later the electricity sputtered and went out.

I was making a fire to keep the house warm for the animals when my cellphone rang. "Hello?" I said pressing it between my shoulder and ear as I scrunched up paper and laid kindling.

"Summer, are you okay?"

"Yes, Jerry, I'm fine. The electricity just went out over here, but I figure it's probably just my street."

"It's out all over town. I wouldn't suggest attempting to get to the store. They're predicting five inches of snow."

"Where are you?"

"I'm at the station. They called me in early because of the storm. This kind of weather seems to lead to shooting deaths and car accidents and all sorts of crazy crap."

"I can understand car accidents, but shooting deaths? Why would that be?"

"I don't know. I guess it's an excuse to bring out your weapons and clean them or something...there is a correlation."

"Weird. I guess I'll stay put if you think the--"

"I don't think, I know. Luckily the station has a back-up generator."

"Thanks for saving me a trip. The car needs new tires, and I'd be taking my life in my hands to try and drive in snow."

"You're welcome. Got to go—Myra needs my expert advice on something." He chuckled and then hung up without saying goodbye.

Myra, with her body that wouldn't quit, her elegant

outfits and wide gray eyes--a sharp feeling of jealousy moved through my body. Damn Jerry to hell! First his mother, and now this woman he'd had an affair with? It didn't matter that she was ten years older, or that the affair happened when Jerry was a cadet, if she had eyes for him he *would* get caught up in her web. Jerry was a sensual guy with an insatiable need to—I let out a scream, startling Cutty. I had to get hold of myself.

After I finished my cappuccino I went to the closet to search for my winter boots. I would walk to Tarot and Tea. The crazy-ass storm with the wind and snow would invigorate me and keep me from dwelling on things I had no control over. Either that or I would be run over by a skidding car, slip in the snow and break a bone, or freeze to death.

"I wondered if you would open today." Mrs. Browning stomped the snow off her boots on the stoop, her gaze on the door I held open. Contrary to Jerry's adamant statement, this part of town had electricity. It flickered once in a while, but so far it held.

I smiled, trying to make up for my behavior the day before. Was that a wary look in the gray-haired woman's eyes? "I wasn't planning to, but since we still have power... beats sitting at home."

"Yes, it does," she agreed, her beady eyes on me. "Did you know I've moved into the Victorian?"

"I didn't know that. Good for you." I watched her,

wondering why she'd brought this up. "Is your power on?"

"Oh yes, dear. Our power never goes out."

I was just about to ask why, when I realized that it must have something to do with the plethora of ghosts living there. I wondered if Agnes even knew how many departed her pet project housed. She was not enamored of specters, only putting up with Douglas because he was her father and seemed so real.

"I'm sorry about your boyfriend," Mrs. Browning said, closing the door behind her. "It seems that your life together has been thrown off course by several issues recently. Don't let it go on for long or you may not get it back," she intoned, her voice trailing off as she disappeared into the shelves.

I hurried after her. "Are you saying he'll pick up with another woman?"

She turned, her eyes widening. "I'm only warning you to not veer off the path any more than you have to, dear. That's all."

"What path? What are you--?"

But my question was interrupted as Valerie Henderson, Becky's mother, emerged through the front door. She shook her umbrella free of snow and stamped her feet. "My, what a lovely day!" she said, looking around brightly. "Is that you, Eleanor?"

Eleanor? This was the first time I'd heard Mrs. Browning's first name. I watched the two of them cackling away as though they were the only people in the world.

A few minutes later Valerie came up to the desk where I sat staring into space. "Eleanor tells me you could use a Tarot card reading, Summer. I'm adept with the cards." She glanced toward the door where snow still fell straight down from the leaden sky. "I don't imagine we'd be interrupted." She turned back, her wide hazel eyes meeting mine. "Becky would approve," she added, smiling. "Especially if we use Lila's old Rider Waite deck."

Did I want a reading? I had no idea. But I did have several pressing questions swirling around my brain. "Maybe I would," I answered. I retrieved the deck from the storeroom window, pulling all the cards into a tidy pile. "Perhaps you'd like to fill my mother's place doing readings in the store?" I said, holding out the deck. A good part of Tarot and Tea's income, when my mother was alive, came from her readings. I could definitely use some extra revenue.

"Ask me that question after I've done a reading for you. You may not like what the cards have to say." She scanned around the store. "Now, where's that old card table Lila used to use?"

I went into the kitchen to retrieve it from where I stashed it after my mother's disappearance. When I brought it out, Valerie had pulled a bright purple scarf out of her pocket and tied it around her hair. I liked the look. "You'd be a perfect addition to the store," I told her, fetching two fold up chairs. I set the card table and chairs up in the shadows behind my desk and found a candle.

She handed me back the deck. "Shuffle," she

ordered.

I worked the cards through my fingers, feeling the ragged edges, the bends in some of them. Mom had used them nearly every day. I tried to organize my thoughts, but they were all over the place. As usual.

Valerie pulled matches out of her pocket and lit the candle. "If someone comes in while we're in the midst of this, what should I do?" she asked, taking the cards I held out.

I shrugged. "Depends who it is. If it's Douglas or another of my regulars keep going, otherwise I'll take a break and deal with them."

Her gaze turned opaque for a moment. "No one will come in," she said decisively as she began placing the cards on the table. She found the page of wands and put it in the center to represent me, and then covered it with another card. Once she had the spread out on the table, she turned over the card 'crossing' me. I saw a frown appear between her penciled in brows. It was the devil.

"What does that mean?"

"There is someone in your life, or close to you, who is trying to subjugate you. But you have the power to remove the bonds."

"There's a naked man and woman there," I said, pointing. "Is that Jerry and me?"

"The cards are not meant to be taken literally, but in this case I might have to say yes. Now, as to what has the chains around your necks, I'm not sure."

I thought immediately of Jerry's mother. "I think I know."

Valerie turned over the second card. "This one is the foundation card, Summer. To figure out the meaning refer back to your original question."

I glanced at the two of cups upside down. "But my question was muddled."

"Muddled? Do you mean vague? Did it have to do with your love-life?"

"I guess so. Jerry and I, we--"

"This can indicate inner conflicts, disharmony in decisions you have made, or are about to make. It can also refer to rash decisions that might lead to problems in the future."

"Mine or someone else's?"

Valerie's clear gaze met mine. "Are you planning something out of the ordinary?"

I thought of Scotland. "Well, I--"

"Could be whatever this is, or it could refer to laying the blame for something on someone else."

I thought of how I'd been treating Jerry since I first thought of going to Scotland. I was rushing forward without discussing it with the one person I shared everything with. And now he was living with his mom.

"This could also refer to a relationship breaking down."

I felt sick for a second. "Can I fix it before it's too late?"

"You may be out of synch with your partner, or maybe your values have changed. Whatever it is represents an imbalance."

"But what should I do?"

Valerie didn't answer as she turned over the next card. "This card represents the recent past."

It was the three of swords, and when I saw the heart pierced with the blades I sucked in my breath. "I don't like the looks of that."

She gazed at me, her eyes filled with sympathy. "This could represent a betrayal or something coming that is unforeseen."

I thought of Jerry at his mother's house—Myra at the station. "I hope it isn't what I think," I muttered, staring at the card.

I heard the tinkle of the bell on the front door, looking up to see Jerry. I jumped up, nearly knocking the table over in my haste. "I can't do any more," I told Valerie, hurrying to where Jerry stood frowning.

I moved close to give him a kiss, but he put his hands up and backed away. "I just got a call from some airline wanting to know if you were going through with the charges on the card."

"What? I haven't made any reservations. I've barely begun to think about the trip"

"If not you then who, Summer? And the charges are on *my* MasterCard. You haven't even discussed it with me!"

"That's ridiculous. I just told you I didn't do this. Are you saying you don't believe me?"

"What am I supposed to believe? I get the call and then…" He glared at me.

"And then, what?"

"And then I find all my clothes packed up in the front room of your cottage, as though you want me out of your hair as soon as possible."

My mouth dropped open. "I would never do that! What's going on?"

He made a face. "Maybe your ghost did it, Summer. How in hell am I supposed to know?"

"Seriously—does this sound like me? Did you leave on bad terms? Don't answer that. We were arguing yesterday, but after you left I sat on the couch and cried because of that damned espresso machine."

"Cried because of the…what are you talking about?"

My eyes filled and I wiped them with my sleeve. "It's a symbol—you know—of our commitment."

"Well, the *symbol*, as you call it, is in the cruiser. I'm taking it to Mom's."

I tried to see his face through my haze of tears. "Jerry, I--"

"I'd like to believe you, Summer, but it isn't plausible that a stranger came into your cottage and packed all my stuff and left it for me to find. And what about the plane ticket? Who would have access to my credit card besides you?"

I shook my head. "I have no idea, but if I find out, I'm going to give him or her a piece of my mind."

"I've removed you from my card. If you want to tell me why you did this, let me know. Mom thinks you're mad because of her, which is unbelievably childish." He turned on his heel and was gone before I could think of an answer, slamming the door behind him.

I opened the door a second later. "Why don't you believe me?" I shouted after him, but he was already opening his car door and didn't turn.

When I closed the door, Mrs. Browning, Valerie and two other customers were staring at me. "That did not sound very cordial, dear," Mrs. Browning said.

"Just like your reading," Valerie added worriedly. She held up the eight of wands. "This is the next card."

"What does that mean?"

"It usually represents an unexpected trip—air travel."

The trip to Scotland that I had no money for? "I didn't do those things, Valerie. Unless a ghost has been messing with my life, something seriously odd is happening," I said, sniffling.

"If you want to close early, please do," an unfamiliar customer said. "The snow has paused for the moment, but I've heard it's supposed to be even worse later."

I gazed blankly at the woman in her late forties, realizing she'd just gotten an earful. "That might be a good idea," I said, trying to get back my self-control. "If anyone would like to purchase anything, please do it in the next half hour."

I headed back to my desk, attempting to swallow the lump in my throat. What must my customers think of me now? I hoped they didn't believe I would use Jerry's credit card without telling him, or that I was the kind of person to basically throw him out of my life. I didn't like the idea of him living with his mom, but I would never punish him over it. Another poisonous tidbit fed to him by his mom. And he believed her.

"Will you be getting any more lavender?" Mrs. Browning asked, coming up with a small bottle of essential oil a few minutes later. "It helps me sleep."

I rang her up. "I don't remember when the shipment is coming, but it should be in the next couple of weeks. That should last you until then." I handed over her change, but instead of leaving the desk, she held my gaze.

"That young man was about to propose, Summer. And now someone has made sure to keep you two apart. I would watch my step if I were you."

"How do you know this, Mrs. Browning?"

She harrumphed and turned away, her bird-like eyes darting around the shop. "It is obvious to the most unskilled observer," she said, depositing the bottle of lavender into her purse. "And I have to say I've heard him several times on the phone attempting to bring it up, but being cut off by you, or something happening on his end."

"You heard…you mean his side of the conversation? How? I didn't have the speaker on."

"I have very good ears, dear. Now try not to fret. I'm sure the universe will fix this situation soon enough. Just make sure not to anger him further before the truth is revealed."

I stared, unable to come up with a question, a comment, or even a reaction. My earlier doubts about her being a ghost were quickly discarded. Before I could think again she had exited the store, the brief moment the door was open revealing several inches of snow on the stoop.

The shop had emptied out during our conversation. Despite not wanting to see my house without Jerry's things in it, it was time for me to head home. I locked up and made my way carefully through the snow, trying not to slip.

CHAPTER SIX

Ames was shut up tight, businesses closed until further notice. I walked by them, a depressed feeling entering my chest. I hadn't heard a weather forecast, but from the low ceiling, this storm could last a while. I thought of a fire and hot chocolate, but without Jerry this would not be nearly as fun. I thought of my reading, the card that pointed to betrayal, and Mrs. Browning's warning. Was someone purposely trying to break us up? Myra's face appeared in my mind, but I couldn't see that sophisticated woman stooping to something like this.

Cutty seemed strangely upset when I came into the cottage, his whining making me wonder if his dog door was blocked. But when I went to check it, all was fine; from the muddy tracks across the kitchen I knew he'd been in and out several times. The cats were both curled up on the couch and barely lifted an eyelid when I came in. Winter cat behavior.

I was sitting on the couch feeling sorry for myself when my cell phone rang. I jumped up to retrieve it from the kitchen counter—it had to be Jerry. But instead of Jerry, it was Agnes.

"I thought you guys weren't coming home until next week."

There was a pause and then Agnes said, "We decided to cut the trip short. I was worried."

"About the baby? Are you feeling okay?"

"I'm fine—just huge. And I do get more tired now. I think Sam was getting antsy too," she whispered.

"He was tired of being in the Bahamas?"

"We've been gone nearly three weeks, Summer. I refused to go snorkeling with him because my bathing suit doesn't fit right, and I got seasick when we went out on the boat, and..." she lowered her voice to a whisper. "He's afraid of hurting me or the baby—he—"

I let out a chuckle. "I don't think he needs to worry. But, Agnes, you aren't due until December, are you?"

"I'm due at the end of November. You should see me—I'm big as a house."

I thought of my ultra-slender friend. "That description does not fit. How much weight have you gained?"

"Twenty five pounds. I'm telling you, I—" There was a pause and then the sound of muffled conversation. A moment later she said, "Jerry just got here. Do you want to come over?"

"My car doesn't have chains, and besides, Jerry just broke up with me."

"What? What happened?"

"I'm sure he'll tell you all about it. But don't believe him. Someone's trying to break us up."

"Gotta go. I'll call tomorrow."

I thought of the three of them together, a pang of hurt jealousy moving through me. Not fair—not fair at all.

I poured wine, staring at the cold fireplace. I forced myself to make a fire, allowing the crackle and spit of the bright flames to cheer me. At least Agnes was home now. Why did Jerry and I always seem to break up right before the holidays?

Morning came way too soon, my sleep disturbed with dreams about Jerry walking away and me chasing him, as he disappeared around one corner after the next. Cutty licked my face, as if to say it was time to get up, but when I glanced out the window it was still snowing. I groaned and rolled over. But when Mischief pounced on my toes, I decided it was time to face the day.

Jerry and I had weathered many break-ups, but for some reason this recent lack of trust seemed worse. Why didn't he believe me? And who had packed up his stuff? No one other than Jerry had a key to my place. Could his mother have done this? It seemed unlikely, considering her broken wrist and advanced age. It gave me a creepy feeling to know that someone had been in my house going through drawers.

Without thinking I headed straight for the espresso machine, letting out a little moan when I saw the empty spot. Fighting tears I stood on a chair to reach in the cabinet for my plunger coffee maker. Once I had a cup of coffee in my hand I pulled open my little notebook and began to make notes about who could be responsible for what had happened.

The first name I put down was his mother, Lucia Brady. She'd hated me from day one. And after Jerry's father committed suicide she'd decided that her baby boy should be at her beck and call at all times. Exasperated, he'd finally hired a woman to live in, but she'd quit after only two months. Jerry's mother was impossible to get along with. I chewed on the pencil.

The scene outside revealed straining tree limbs bent with the weight of the snow. I wondered if any of my customers had decided to brave the weather. I turned back to my notebook. Myra Proctor was name two, but I had a strong feeling that it couldn't be her. For one thing she hadn't exhibited any romantic interest in Jerry. Yes, they'd been together in the past, but that was when they were both young and foolish. It had to be his mother— she was the only one who had access to his credit card number. I put a little star next to her name.

And if he'd left his keys on the table in her hallway, she could have used them to get into my cottage, or possibly hired someone to do her dirty work. Having a chief of police for a husband must have acquainted her with many off- duty or retired cops she could call. I found myself doodling a female face with horns. I was suddenly furious, jumping up from the table to search for my phone. I had to vent to someone. But before I could punch in the numbers, it rang.

"Hi," Agnes said tentatively.

"I was just about to call you."

"I beat you to it!" she said with false brightness.

"Well? What did he say?"

"Jerry? He told us about the credit card, Summer. I can't believe you didn't ask him first."

I was speechless for a moment. "Agnes, I told you not to believe him! I did not use his damn credit card."

"He said you were the only other person on it. Who else could it have been?"

I was fuming now. "His mother is the only person I can think of. And whoever did this also got into my house and packed up all his stuff."

"Yeah, he mentioned that too. He was really hurt. He said you were pissed because he had to help out his mother while her arm's healing."

"And you believe him over me."

"Honestly, I don't know what to believe. I know you hate his mom."

"I can't believe you'd take his side. I thought you knew me."

"I do know you. I have to say that it doesn't sound like you—especially the credit card thing, but you and Jerry have had your ups and downs."

Tears filled my eyes. "I love Jerry. I was upset when he decided to spend time with his mom, but I'd never kick him out because of it."

There was a long silence as I searched for a tissue to blow my nose. "Are you still there?" I asked.

"He told us about the ghost in the graveyard. He said you've been obsessed with him."

"I haven't been obsessed. I told Jerry that my relative wants me to find out who murdered him."

"And it would mean a trip to Scotland by yourself."

"So what? Jerry and I aren't attached at the hip. But bottom line, I don't have the money for it, anyway."

There was a pause and then she said, "If you really want to go I can lend you the money. I have plenty of it."

Agnes had inherited a small fortune after Serena was poisoned—an unexpected windfall. "I can't do that!"

"Why not? It's not like I did anything to inherit all that money. And maybe you going off on your own will get Jerry to open his eyes for a change."

"So you do believe me."

She sighed. "Jerry is a hot-headed Italian who overreacts. This thing with his mother would drive anyone crazy."

"What all did he say?"

"He's beyond it, Summer. Even Sam said he was being unreasonable. Did something else happen?"

"Besides his mother setting me up?"

"When Sam took your side, Jerry just shut him down. He seems to be looking for a reason to be mad at you."

"His mother's very manipulative. She's probably convinced him that I'm a gold digger or something. Why does she hate me so much?"

"Isn't Jerry the youngest? He's her baby. Until he finds a way to stand up to her, you guys don't have much of a future."

My heart sank as I took in the truth of her words. "I think you're right. And I just decided to take you up on your offer. Getting away sounds good right now."

"I'll only give you the money if you promise to be back in time for the birth. I'm not going into the hospital without you there."

"You have Sam."

"I need you. Do you promise?"

"If I go soon there won't be any problem. I figure I'll only be gone a week or so."

"Do you want me to watch the store?"

"Becky said she'd find someone, but if you want to—"

"I kinda do. I'll go crazy for the next month if I'm not busy. If I don't feel well maybe Becky can call whoever she has in mind?"

"I'll check with her. Thanks, Agnes. I feel better knowing you're in my corner."

"Come by today after work, okay? I'll give you a glass of wine and we can figure out the details for the flight."

"I'll be there if the snow ever stops. I'd better get going or I'll be late for work."

"Check into flights today. The sooner you go the sooner you'll be back. Hope to see you later."

As soon as I hung up I thought about Cutty and the cats. Without Jerry I would have to find someone to stay at the house. Becky was single—maybe she wouldn't mind doing it. Was I actually planning a trip to Scotland?

CHAPTER SEVEN

The day went by in a blur, my mind on the trip. At lunch I hurried down to the bakery to see if Becky would mind staying at the house. "I'd love to!" she answered immediately.

One less thing to worry about, I thought, as I took money and fielded questions about essential oils, books that I didn't have in stock, and Tarot decks I didn't know about. I jotted down people's wants, vowing to order the missing items as soon as possible. By the time five o'clock rolled around I was ready to leave, my mind on the glass of wine Agnes promised, and discussing my trip plans, and how to manage it all.

Luckily the snow had dissipated, the streets wet, but no longer frozen. My bald tires didn't slip once as I drove up the hill to Agnes's house. I had my hand out to knock when the door opened, revealing my friend's ivory-pale face. She smiled and reached to give me a hug, crushing me against her enormous belly. Once we were inside I looked her over. "Are you sure your due date is right?"

"That's what I've been telling you!" She held her arms out and twirled to show her body off. "I'm an elephant, right?"

I laughed. "Hardly, Agnes. But I suggest you get

checked out before I take off for Scotland. Maybe they got the date wrong."

"I have an appointment tomorrow morning—Sam insisted."

"Is he worried?"

"He wants to make sure things are all right. You know Sam. He's a worrywart. And when I mentioned your trip he was doubly insistent."

"He wants me there."

Agnes nodded. "I have a feeling he's going to be like one of those past generation fathers who either go to a movie, or pace the halls smoking." She giggled. "I'll get no help from the man once the contractions start."

"I hadn't pegged him for such a sissy."

"He's terrified, Summer. He can't stand the idea of me in pain. He treats me like a princess."

"I had noticed that. Now where's that glass of wine you promised me?"

She waddled to the kitchen and retrieved the already poured glass, handing it over. "Wish I could have one," she whined, pouting.

I took a sip and watched her lower herself to the couch. It was very strange to see my ultra-skinny friend with a belly this big. She was wearing an old black sweater over tights, the loops of wool stretched to full capacity. "I won't make any plans until we know for sure when this baby is coming."

"Did you call about flights?"

"I found out the few that would work, but I didn't make a reservation yet. How shall we do this?"

"I'll put the ticket on my card. But what about your accommodations once you're over there?"

"I have enough to pay for that and food. I have to get some more information from Finlay. I don't know anything at all about the murderer, or where I should look for him."

"Isn't your mission to discover the murderer?"

"Yes, but I'm sure Finlay has several names to share." I stared into space, thinking about the last time I'd been to the graveyard. "I guess I better go talk with him tonight."

Agnes shuddered. "You are way braver than I am."

"Who crawled into that cave with me to find the skeleton?" I asked, my mind going to the last case Jerry and I worked on together.

"If I'd known what we'd find I never would have gone in."

I laughed, thinking about her ear-piercing shriek when I held up the human femur bone.

When Sam arrived a few minutes later I gulped down the rest of my wine. "Let me know what the doctor says," I called, heading for the door. But before I reached it Sam came up and hugged me.

"Don't think for a moment I believe you did those things," he whispered.

"Thanks, Sam. That makes me feel better. Did you tell Jerry?"

"I did, but it didn't make much difference. Have you met his mother? Seems like she rules the roost and all her chicks."

"Agnes said that if he didn't learn to stand up to her, we were doomed."

"I wouldn't go that far. He loves you, Summer."

"And I love him. But what difference does it make when he believes this crap about me?"

"I'll keep talking to him." He gave my arm a squeeze before closing the door.

I headed to my car, caught up in my feelings for Jerry. Damn the man! If I'd planned this right Jerry and I could both be heading on this adventure. Instead he was living with his mother, and seemed to have decided I was a thieving conniving bitch.

It was very dark by the time I reached the cottage, but at least the snow hadn't started up again. I fed Cutty and the cats and retrieved my warm coat from the closet. I stuffed a small notebook and a pen into a pocket of my coat and glanced out the window. The clouds had parted, leaving a bitterly cold star-filled sky--the perfect time to talk with Finlay. I only hoped he wouldn't disappear before he filled me in on exactly what I should look for.

Cutty finished his food and was at the door before I'd opened it. "You want to go with me again? It's cold out there." He wagged his tail. I fished his leash from the closet floor and clicked it to his collar. "Come on then."

The graveyard was even spookier than the last time I'd been, shadows racing across the gravestones as clouds moved by. The stars were suddenly obscured, and with the moon in its dark phase and the skeleton trees, a cold shiver of fear moved up my spine. Unlike the ones in my store, the ghosts in the graveyard were an unknown.

I pulled out my phone and turned on the flashlight, making my way carefully around the leaning moss covered stones until I reached Finlay's grave. "Finlay? Are you here? I need to talk to you," I whispered, trying not to notice the specters wafting about.

He appeared a second later, doffing his cap in welcome. "Are ye planning yer trip, lass?"

Although he wasn't solid, I still breathed a sigh of relief, heartened by his presence. "I am, but I need more details before I go. Who do you think killed you, and is he here in the graveyard?"

"He is nae here. As far as who he is, could be one of two lads—Frank Mackenzie or Ian Camran. Neither one had much love for me. But my bet is on Ian, since it was the lassie he was after."

"I didn't find any record of your death at the library. Are you sure you were killed here?"

Confusion flickered across his translucent features. "I'm in a grave here, lass. Yer questions are gratin' on me now."

I watched him for a moment. "I still don't get it, Finlay. Why do you want me to travel all the way to Scotland? Did the man who killed you go back?"

Finlay froze, his gaze swinging into the darkness. "He must have. We were all friends, but when Ian's lass fell in love with me, and we married, he turned bitter." There was a long silence before he added, "I could nae help that she loved me, now could I?"

When he grinned, the light revealed how handsome and charming he must have been. Cutty gave a little woof, looking up at my distant relative.

"Elspeth bore me three children," he continued, "before I was taken from this world. I never got to see 'em grown. I want ye to check for any remaining McClouds. I wish to know how they fared, ye ken?"

"Do you think your children moved back to Scotland? I didn't see much in the way of McClouds in the museum or the library. Mom said she was born here, so there must have been at least one."

Finlay ran a hand across his chin. "Maybe they..." his voice drifted off.

I used the ensuing silence to jot down names in my notebook. "So I need to search for Elspeth McCloud, Ian Camran and Frank Mackenzie. And what are your children's names?"

"Sara, Ross, and Finlay."

I printed the names next to the others, making a note to find their descendants. "Two boys, then. One of them must have stayed. Unless Mom's descended from another part of the McCloud line."

"Best if ye concentrate on who killed me. As much as I like talkin' to ye, I feel there is another life waitin' for me outside this graveyard."

"Is there anyone else in Scotland who could help me? I mean I know they're all dead now, but someone whose relatives might still be living?"

"The names I gave ye are all prominent families, lass. Their descendants will still be there." Finlay stared into the distance, his pale eyes clouding. The confusion was back on his face.

I gazed into the shadows where translucent shapes wafted as though eavesdropping. "It seems there are a lot of you in the same predicament."

Finlay followed my gaze. "Some dinna wish to move on, and the others…wish to do harm."

"Do harm? How can ghosts…?"

But Finlay looked suddenly frightened, his eyes wide as he squinted into the dark. "'Tis evil, lass." A moment later he was gone.

He'd seemed oddly bewildered this time. Maybe that's what happened after you'd been dead for over a hundred years. And how could a ghost be evil? I'd seen silly movies depicting ghosts who were doing harm, but without being corporeal, how was it possible? But then I thought of Douglas. He seemed as real as anyone else I knew.

Not for the first time, I wished Mom were alive. With her witchy psychic sense she would have given me more to go on, and maybe even come along on the trip. I felt hollow for a moment. It had been nearly seven years since her death, but still I mourned her loss.

I pulled my dog away from where he stared at Finlay's headstone, and hurried out of the graveyard to the cottage.

When I got home I took a hot shower to warm up. Once I had on my warmest pj's, I made some dinner and sat in the living room, my mind conjuring wild landscapes and ancient standing stones with ghosts wafting around them. When my thoughts went to Jerry I turned them to other matters. I would not let him divert me from this crazy adventure I was about to embark on.

As soon as I heard from Agnes in the morning I would call and get my plane ticket. There was no point in going over and over what was happening with Jerry. The man would either realize he was being a fool, or not. If his mother had this much sway over him, there was no way our relationship could grow. Best to get on with my life and accept that he was no longer a part of it. I wiped at the tears that threatened, telling myself to get over it— that it was a good thing this was happening now. But part of me didn't buy that glib assessment.

CHAPTER EIGHT

It was noon and no one was in the store—the perfect moment to call Agnes and find out her news. I punched in her numbers. "Well?" I asked.

"The due date is November twenty-fifth, but she said I may have to be induced. The baby is huge already and my hips are narrow."

"When would that happen?"

"Sometime in mid November, if nothing changes."

"Today is November fifth. That gives me plenty of time. If I go now there shouldn't be a problem, right?"

There was a pause, and then Agnes, sounding a bit wan, answered. "I would feel better if you got back as soon as possible."

"What worries you—being induced?"

"The size could be an indication of something being wrong, Summer. Why did he grow this fast? And why would I have a baby inside me who is too big to birth naturally? I've been counting on a natural birth. I don't want all that doctor stuff and instruments—it freaks me out!"

"If it's a boy they're naturally bigger. Maybe Sam's genes took over. His family is enormous compared to you. Did the doctor say something to worry you?"

"All she said was that if he reaches a certain size she would recommend inducing him or doing a cesarean. But she's also been very supportive about a natural birth."

"Would you rather I didn't go?"

"No. But just please don't stay away long."

"What will you name him?"

"Samuel, same as his father. Can you go this week? That way you'll for sure be back in time."

"I'll look and see what's available and give you a ring back. But you'll need to call the airlines with your credit card number." I glanced up when several customers arrived. "Got to go. And don't worry!" I clicked off just as Valerie arrived at my desk, a worried frown on her face.

"How are your trip plans going?" she asked.

"I haven't finalized them yet."

"Do you want to hear about the last card in your reading?"

"Probably not by the look on your face."

"All the reading does is help you with upcoming events. It's never set in stone."

I sighed. "Okay. What was it?"

She held out the Lovers card. "In the context of the reading I find this a disturbing card, Summer."

"Because Jerry and I are on the outs?"

"In a reading of this nature it can mean an affair of the heart and conflict between two lovers. Be careful over there."

"On that note I need to call the airlines and get a seat." My pulse raced. An affair? With Jerry being a jackass it seemed fitting, but I would never want to hurt him like that.

I looked up the airline on my phone and hit *call*, watching Valerie head toward Mrs. Browning. When I glanced up again they were both watching me with worry in their eyes. For gods sakes! Couldn't I do anything without all my customers being involved?

I got the information I needed and quickly called Agnes, glad when she sounded a bit more upbeat.

"I spoke with Sam and he told me one of his sisters had this exact problem. Everything went fine with her, and she was able to give birth naturally."

"I'm glad to hear that, Agnes. I'm texting you my information so you can pay. Is that okay?"

"Absolutely. What day are you going?"

"This is Wednesday, right? The flight is on Friday." A flutter of nerves went through my stomach, my pulse heading into overdrive.

"Friday! Good. I'll get back to you later."

"Thanks so much, Agnes. Without you I wouldn't be able to do this at all."

"Did you talk with the ghost again?"

"I did. I have three names to look up while I'm there." I glanced at Valerie before whispering, "And apparently there was a card in my Tarot reading that indicated an affair."

"Really? The way Jerry's been acting that might be kind of fun for you."

"I don't think it would help us in the long run—that is if there still is an 'us'. He hasn't called."

"Sam will let me know what's going on with him. Right now you need to concentrate on packing. I'm excited for you."

I thanked her again, said goodbye and disconnected, barely able to think. In two days I would be flying off to a foreign country!

"Have a good trip, dear," Mrs. Browning called before she left the store. How she knew I'd made my final plans was anyone's guess. Ghosts seemed to be able to read minds, hear with preternatural acuity, and know things before they happened.

Valerie stopped by my desk a while later. "Please heed my warning, Summer. What I saw in your reading points to some odd happenings. I wouldn't want you to get lost out there in the wilds of Scotland."

"Lost? I thought you said a possible affair!"

Valerie glanced away for a second before she answered. "There were several other cards we didn't get to. They seemed to suggest some otherworldly involvements."

"I am going over to find some ghosts, specifically the one who killed my distant relative."

"This is more than that. Just please be careful."

As she left the store I had a premonition of eerie darkness, shadowy ruins, specters running amok, and the rumble of thunder in the distance. What was I getting myself into?

"You'll be fine," a male voice said, startling me. I turned to see Douglas, standing next to me. "Valerie tends to be overly dramatic," he explained. "You are a sensible girl and very intuitive. You'll do fine amongst the standing stones and the relics of the ages." He smiled.

"Thanks, Douglas. She kind of freaked me out."

"Enjoy your trip with all its vagaries. It should prove very interesting." With that cryptic statement he turned away and headed toward the door. And this time he didn't bother to open it, gliding through with ghost-like precision.

I quickly glanced around to make sure no one else had seen him. But the only other customers were far from the door with their heads in books. The word, vagaries, seemed oddly sinister, but then again, chasing down ghosts could be placed in that category.

I spent the next half hour looking into a hotel reservation, settling on a town called Dornoch, a seaside resort that sat along the north shore of the Dornoch firth in Sutherland. The places further north seemed too small to have much in the way of inns or hotels. The pictures I found of Dornoch showed a medium-sized pleasant town, with a golf course and long empty beaches, not that I would be sunbathing at this time of year. Very picturesque. When I looked up hotels I found an inexpensive one called the Dornoch Inn. I was able to make my reservation on line.

By the time I'd finished with my plans, the store had emptied out, the clock showing ten minutes to five. I was beginning to get my receipts in order when the door flew open and Jerry strode in. His face was the color of cooked beets, his hair tousled from the wind.

"I want you to stay out of my life!" he shouted, his hands balling into fists.

"What did I do now?"

"As if you don't know!" He took a deep breath, obviously trying to calm

himself down. "My sister told me you texted her, suggesting that my mother was harassing you."

"Which sister? I've only met them once at your dad's funeral."

"Don't play coy with me, Summer. This is the last straw. Just leave me the fuck alone!"

Before I could answer he'd turned on his heel, heading back toward the wide open door where leaves were blowing in by the bucket load. A second later it slammed behind him, rattling the glass. I sat there in a daze for several minutes before the ring of my phone brought me out of it.

"Summer?" Agnes said. "Are you there?"

"Barely. Jerry just came by and accused me of more stuff. Who is doing this?"

"What now?"

"Texting one of his sisters and telling her his mother is harassing me. For one thing I don't know his sisters, and for another, why would I do that?"

"Sam says Jerry's been acting bizarre ever since he moved in with her. Could his mother be behind this?"

"To break us up for good? Yes, I think she could."

"Sam told me that..." she paused.

"What...what did Sam say?"

"Jerry had a date last night with some gal his mom

knows. Apparently she's the daughter of a friend."

The blood drained from my head. "She's trying to fix him up? That utter bitch!"

"Try not to think about it. If he chooses to believe her over you, there's nothing you can do. I called to tell you I got the tickets taken care of. I emailed the information."

I barely heard her, my mind consumed with Lucia Brady. What had I ever done to her to deserve this treatment?

"Summer, are you still there?"

"I'm sorry, Agnes. Thanks for the tickets. I just can't believe this is happening."

"Until she's out of the picture, or he learns to believe you over her, you may as well give up."

"Perfect time for me to get away for a few days."

"He'll come to his senses, Summer."

"At this moment I don't care whether I ever see him again. I thought he loved me!"

"He does. He's just been bewitched by his mother."

"That's a good way of putting it, but the word 'witch' is too good for her."

"Why don't you come over for dinner tonight. It might cheer you up."

"No. I have too much to do before I go. But thanks."

I was still seething by the time I got home, my hands shaking as I put the key into the lock. I wanted to call him, but I was afraid he would either hang up on me, or rage some more. And if he was at his mother's house…no. I had to get a grip and let him go his own way. Whatever was going on would come to light eventually. And if it didn't—well—then I had to think that Jerry and I weren't meant to be. A second after this thought went through my mind I was crying. And the tears continued for a very long time. Had Mrs. Browning been right—was he really about to propose? And if so, how could his mother sway him so quickly? That woman was evil incarnate.

I was calmly drinking wine and planning what to pack when my phone rang. It was Agnes again. "Just wanted to tell you that Jerry had no interest in the woman."

"Well, thank goodness for small favors," I quipped, taking a gulp of wine. "I'm sure Lucia Brady will find some other suitable wife for her precious boy."

"Sam says the man's lost without you. You're like his compass, and now he's all over the place."

"Glad to hear it. Too bad Jerry doesn't see it."

"Will we see you before you go?"

"I doubt it. I still have a ton of things to do to get ready. And to tell you the truth, I'm shattered. I can't visit right now."

"At least call me, okay? Can you call while you're there?"

"I'm not sure. But if I can I will. You're my best friend," I said, my voice breaking. "I feel like I've been set adrift on a dark sea in a boat without oars or a rudder."

"It's going to be okay. Jerry overreacts to stuff. He's

had his share of mental issues."

"That's what worries me. If he finds out his mother is a conniving bitch he'll never get over it. Maybe it's better that he blames it all on me."

"He needs you, Summer. Don't give up on him."

"Me? He's the one who's given up on me."

We hung up a moment later and I began to cry again. It felt like my heart was breaking as I pictured him storming into my store and accusing me of things I would never do. Cutty jumped up on the couch next to me, his soulful eyes staring into mine. I hugged him and let my tears fall into the wiry ruff around his neck. A few minutes later I donned my coat and headed for the graveyard.

I was sitting on the ground next to his grave crying, when Finlay appeared. "What is it, lass?"

"My boyfriend's mother is breaking us up."

"Aye. 'Tis the way with some mothers...they think they know best for their laddies."

I wiped the tears from my eyes. "Did that happen to you?"

He nodded. "Elspeth was my choice, the love o' me life, but my mam had another in mind."

"I'm sorry. What happened with you?"

He shook his head, his eyes going sad. "I never laid eyes on her again. She brought it on herself. The woman was as stubborn as they come."

"What about your father?"

"He died early. Yer man will see the light, lass. I saw how he looked at ye."

I stood and brushed off my pants. "As long as you're here I have one more question. Why do you think you were stabbed?"

"The murder weapon? Seemed fittin' since I was in the metal-craftin' business, I suppose. My family and Ian's were all in the same business. Ye'd best check out the Camrans." He let out a soft chuckle.

"I should have looked for a knife or a dagger in the museum while I was there. Where do you think the weapon got to?"

He shrugged. "Here, there? 'Tis anyone's guess."

A moment later he was gone. I saw the strange glow on the other side of the graveyard, wondering for the second time what Finlay was afraid of. Maybe someone from his past was buried here, and had a 'bone to pick', I thought, chuckling. But I could feel the malevolent energy from whatever it was, and had a sudden urge to be out of here.

I spent a restless night worrying about Jerry's recent behavior, and my upcoming trip, waking in the morning with a splitting headache. When my phone rang I stumbled into the kitchen to answer.

"If you want to spend the day getting packed and ready I can watch the shop," Agnes said.

"Thanks, Agnes, but I need to write you some notes and make sure you can figure things out before I leave."

"Are you okay?"

"I didn't sleep that well, but yes, I'm fine."

"Sam is furious with Jerry, if that makes you feel any

better."

I laughed. "Actually, it does."

"Who's driving you to the airport?"

"I am. I'm leaving my car in the long term lot."

I hung up a moment later and made coffee, still mourning the loss of Jerry's machine. Maybe I would buy one of my own—that is, when I had enough money saved up. This trip would deplete what little savings I had, not to mention paying Agnes back. I wondered what kind of payment plan we could work out.

I was driving to the shop when I saw a police cruiser behind me with the lights flashing. I wasn't speeding, but I pulled over, hoping it would drive past, but it didn't. When the officer arrived at my window I smiled. "Hi Sam. I wasn't speeding, was I?"

He laughed, blue eyes crinkling at the corners. "No. I wanted to wish you bon voyage, and let you know that I'm keeping a close eye on Jerry."

"Thanks, Sam. I'm sure it's his mother who's doing all of this. I don't understand why she hates me so much."

"I don't know her well, but I don't think she likes women. Her daughters have complained bitterly about how she treats them."

"Except for the one who said I texted her."

Sam scoffed. "Lucia has a plethora of unsavory friends to call on. Her husband, the chief, had his fingers in many pies before his dismissal from the force."

"So someone she knows used my phone number to text her daughter?"

"Easy enough if you know what you're doing."

I shook my head wearily. "Glad I'm getting out of here for a while."

Sam leaned in to give me a kiss. "Just make sure you get back before the baby comes. I can't go through the birth alone."

I laughed. "You can hunt down criminals, shoot people, drag people off to jail, but you can't support your wife while she gives birth?"

He grimaced. "The idea of that woman in pain does something to my insides."

"I promise to be here, Sam. And thanks for the kind words. I hope Jerry and I have a future, but right now it seems rather remote."

"Have a good trip, Summer."

I waited for him to drive past before I pulled back into traffic. I couldn't believe my original dislike of this man; he was sweet, kind and generous, and right now I envied my friend more than I cared to admit.

CHAPTER NINE

I was shaking with excitement and nerves when I boarded the plane. When I found my seat I was gratified to find that it was next to a window. I sat and pushed my carry-on under the seat in front of me, glancing around at other passengers doing the same. On the other side of the tiny window the sky had turned a menacing shade of gray. I hoped snow and ice wouldn't prevent us from taking off.

I mentally went over everything at home, ticking off the notes to Agnes, the notes to Becky about the animals, and my assurances to call once I settled into the hotel. I had also lined up a car--so much for the rest of my savings. Too bad ghosts couldn't give advances when they wanted mysteries solved.

For a second my mind drifted into a fantasy about becoming a modern day Agatha Christie—traveling around the world to solve crimes. So far I'd seen no money for my sleuthing—it was Jerry who always took the credit, except for the one case when he totally lost it.

When an older woman sat down next to me I was struck with the hardness in her piercing blue eyes. She turned away without saying hello and pulled a book out of her bag. I stared out the window, trying to hide my uneasiness.

Despite my excitement I fell asleep shortly after takeoff, my head lolling against the window. I must have been more tired than I realized. The loudspeaker roused me later, announcing our imminent arrival in London. "Did I sleep through the entire flight?" I asked the woman, rubbing the sleep from my eyes.

She turned her bland gaze to mine. "Yes," was all she said before pressing her book, *How to communicate with ghosts,* back into her bag.

Okay, the ghost book was a strange coincidence. From her unfriendly aura I decided not to ask about it. I put my mind on what I had to do once I got off the plane.

I'd booked a seat on Ryanair for the short hop up to Glasgow. From there I would rent a car and drive to Dornoch. I had no idea how long it would take to get there. Now all I had to do was retrieve my bags, and find out where the other gate might be. I figured by tonight I'd be about dead on my feet.

I was frazzled by the time I collected my bag and walked what seemed like an endless maze of corridors scanning signs for Ryanair. It was still early morning and the next flight didn't leave until after ten. I had to change some money before I left the airport, and after missing the meal on the flight over, the signs pointing to food were enticing. I dragged my bag, bumping after me, and headed down yet another long corridor.

It was nine fifteen by the time I found my flight and

settled on an orange plastic chair to wait. Jet lag was encroaching, but I felt better after my mocha and the sausage bap. And I was very glad I'd spent the flight sleeping. Jerry entered my mind, his face red with anger. "Go away," I muttered. And he did.

The voices around me twanged with the curving vowels of British and Scottish English. The clothes and hairstyles were dissimilar too, and the faces were not like U.S. faces. But how was hard to pinpoint. I even heard what I thought was Italian being spoken. It seemed the wrong time of year for holiday goers to be heading north.

It was then that I noticed the woman from the flight over, her haughty gaze scanning across the rest of the waiting crowd. I remembered her book, wondering if this was one of the 'vagaries' Douglas had mentioned. I turned away, too excited about what was happening to be concerned with her. I couldn't believe I was sitting in the airport in London about to head off to the Highlands of Scotland.

Scotland had always been a land of mystery to me, with misty emerald glens, ancient standing stones, faeries, and other magical creatures that lived under rocks and in trees. My meandering thoughts were cut short when the flight was announced. I moved into the small line of people boarding, the sound of my pulse loud in my ears.

An hour and twenty minutes later we were over Glasgow, high winds buffeting the plane as it came in for a landing. The sky was charcoal gray, unfamiliar architecture in the distance giving me a little thrill. We bounced and rolled along quickly before coming to an abrupt stop. Now all I had to do was find my rental and drive into the wilds of the countryside. I was sure it would be dark before I reached Dornoch, that is if I didn't get confused and run off the road and land in a ditch.

"What do you mean you don't have any cars?" I asked the red-haired woman behind the car rental counter. "I reserved one."

"I am sorry, my dear, but ye never know what may happen this time o' year."

I got so caught up in her brogue that I barely registered what she said. "But—what should I do?"

"Where are ye travelin'?"

"Dornoch."

Her eyebrows pulled together. "My brother lives in Dornoch and happens to be headin' home. I could call to see if he'd mind givin' ye a ride." She must have noticed my skeptical expression because she quickly added, "He's a trustworthy older gentleman."

"Okay," I finally said, weighing my options.

She nodded. "I'll just give him a call."

I sat down to wait, watching her turn her back and speak softly into the phone. At one point she turned to look at me and then turned away again. I was staring at the floor, feeling my fatigue coming on, when I heard her voice.

"He should be here in fifteen minutes."

"What should I pay him?"

She waved her hand in the air. "He's headed there anyway. I doubt he will need any money from ye."

The wind had begun to howl, sheets of rain slanting sideways across the road. When I saw an older man running toward the building I rose. "Is that your brother?"

"Aye. That's Ian now."

I grabbed my bags and hurried to the door just as he opened it. He took one look at me and smiled. "Ye must be the American lass my sister told me about."

"I'm Summer McCloud," I said, holding out my hand.

He grabbed my fingers. "Ian Camran."

My mouth dropped open in surprise. This name was on my list. He looked to be around fifty. Could he be related to the Ian Camran Finlay mentioned? Maybe it was just an odd coincidence.

He had kind blue eyes in a lined face, gray hair curling around the cap he wore. Any reservations I'd had about him had already disappeared. He waved to his sister and grabbed my heavier bag and hurried to his car, me following quickly on his heels.

A few minutes later we were heading through the rain, avoiding oncoming cars that seemed to be driving on the wrong side of the road. "Is rain normal for this time of year?"

He laughed. "Any kind of weather is normal for these parts. And if the wind stops blowin', everyone falls down."

I laughed, watching branches flailing wildly as we drove past. I would need more rain gear, a pair of Wellies. Would ghosts be willing to come out if it was raining? I chuckled to myself.

"The trip to Dornoch will take about four hours, lass. If ye wish to nap there's a rug in back to keep out the chill."

"Four hours? I'm glad they didn't have my car; with this weather I never would have made it." I gazed out the window for a while and then asked, "Is there a place in Dornoch where I could find a list of the old families? I may have some relatives living up in Sutherland."

"Ach—lots of Macleods up north." We left the city behind and turned onto an A road heading northwest.

"How far from Dornoch?"

"Check in the local museum and ask about Clan Macleod. They will know where to point ye."

I watched the traffic moving past on the right, unable to wrap my mind around it. "Could I hire you to drive me around once we get up there? I don't much fancy the idea of driving on the wrong side of the road."

The gray haired man chuckled. "The wrong side, eh?"

I smiled. "You know what I mean."

"There is nae much traffic in those parts, but if ye wish it, I have the time."

"I would pay you like any driver for hire."

He looked out the window, his brows pulling together. "An entire day or part of the day?"

"Probably half days—sometimes mornings and sometimes afternoons? I'll be in Dornoch for a week."

"Ninety pound for the week."

I counted it up in my head, figuring it was a

reasonable charge, and less than I would have paid for the car. And now I wouldn't have to take my life into my hands with the steering wheel on the right and driving on the left. "What if I want to visit a ruin or two at night?"

"At night?" He swung his gaze to me. "Why would ye wish that?"

I smiled. "It's a long story that involves ghosts."

He shook his head, his eyebrows rising. "As long as I'm in my bed before the wee hours, and ye dinna have me stuck in mud on some dirt track in the wilds."

"You know where to go to find ghosts?"

"If it's a graveyard yer after, there are a few about."

"The Clan McCloud ghosts, maybe?"

He frowned. "That would require a longer trip. Ardvreck Castle, built by Clan Macleod, could be what yer lookin' for. But 'tis a lonely stretch, and bein' up there after dark does nae please me."

"We can go during the day."

He didn't say anything, his gaze in the distance where the rain had turned into a heavy mist. Despite the time of year, the pastures we drove past were green and lush. Small white washed cottages hugged the hills, stonewalls that had seen better days, tumbled around them. There were newer farms as well, with silos and better fencing to hold in the sheep and fuzzy red-brown Highland cattle that were munching on grass or lying down.

We chatted about this and that for a while. His wife had died early on, and two daughters lived in Edinburgh. His one son was still in Dornoch. Despite my protestations about being too excited to sleep I did doze for about an hour.

When I woke we were on a remote stretch of highway. "How close are we?" I asked, rubbing my eyes. The landscape we drove by was less hilly, black-faced sheep with curled horns grazing in clusters here and there. The walls made of stone were works of arts, and built higher to keep the sheep in. The rain persisted.

"We are past Inverness now. Another hour or so to Dornoch, I'd say. I know a place we can get a wee bite if yer hungry."

"Unless you want to stop, I'm fine. I have a reservation at the Dornoch Inn. Do you know it?"

"The owner, Mairi Flynn, is a friend o' mine. She'll take good care o' ye."

What business are you, or were you, in?"

"My ancestors were blade smiths, but now we make more daggers and knives than swords, although we still have the occasional order for one. I'm semi-retired, but my son has taken over most of the day-to-day runnin' o' the business. 'Tis why I can gallivant all over and give attractive young ladies rides up into the wilds of the Highlands."

I laughed. "Would your ancestors have made a dagger or a knife that could kill a man?"

He glanced at me quickly. "Aye. We made swords and all manner of daggers, claymores, and the like."

"I heard that the Camrans and the McClouds were partners way back when."

He nodded. "The venture did nae last long. The

Camrans bought them out. But that was back in the 1700's, lass. How did ye hear about it? The business is small and nae famous."

"Maybe I read about it in a history book," I lied. "Did any of your relatives go to Ames, Connecticut?"

"Ames, ye say? Never heard of it."

"Have you heard of Finlay Ross McCloud? His wife was Elspeth and his children were Sara, Ross and Finlay."

"There was a Finlay Macleod here way before my time, lived up north a ways. As I said, their family and my family were close back then. We shared the business."

"Not now?"

He smiled. "Kind of like your infamous Hatfields and McCoys--feudin' ever since."

"I heard that Finlay and a man named Ian Camran fell in love with the same gal."

Ian chuckled. "That was my very distant relative many generations ago. Those stories were told to me when I was a lad. Finlay won her hand in the end."

"Did that distant relative of yours murder Finlay?"

Ian jerked to face me. "Havna heard that one— where'd ye get that?"

I sighed, not willing to tell him I could talk to ghosts. "Some McCloud history that was written down by my family—you don't think it's true?"

He shrugged and swerved to miss a sheep that had managed to get loose. "Tis an old story, lass. Finlay died around 1810 and was buried somewhere out on the moors. Elspeth, his wife, lived on with her two children. If I recall my history one of 'em moved to America."

"I have a McCloud relative in the graveyard in Ames who died in 1884."

"What is the first name?"

"Finlay Ross McCloud."

"Must have been the son. The Finlay who married Elsbeth was born sometime in the 1760's, if memory serves."

When I pictured Finlay's gravestone, the dates of 1789—1884 loomed into my mind, as clear as bold printing on a page. The man buried there had been ninety-five. Finlay looked around forty-five or fifty, and from what I'd noticed, ghosts remained the age they'd been the day they died. I frowned, puzzling over this. "How do you know so much about the past?" I finally asked.

He chuckled. "Ancestry is a hobby of mine, and with the feud between the Camrans and the Macleods, it makes for interestin' readin'."

I thought about my Finlay, wondering if he was the earlier one and didn't know it. Had the son moved on and the father had become stuck due to being murdered? It would explain his confusion. I wanted to ask Ian, but couldn't do it without giving myself away. When I glanced over at him, his gaze was on the rain slick road ahead, a frown of concentration puckering his forehead. "Are you okay? I feel bad not spelling you."

"I'm just fine, lass. It's only that my eyes grow tired when I'm starin' into the rain, not that it's anythin' new, ye ken."

By the time we reached the Dornoch Inn I was feeling dizzy and off balance. The rain had turned into a light drizzle, and clouds now raced across the very dark sky. When I stepped out of the car I detected the tangy salt of the sea, the ocean mist coating my skin. I breathed in, looking forward to a walk by the water.

Ian carried my bag into the modern lobby, the grays and blacks and large mirrors reflecting the dull colors outside. I imagined a splash of orange here and there, thinking it would enliven the place a bit. After my perusal I saw Ian in conversation with the man at the desk.

When I reached the dark marble counter he was turning to go. "Mairi will be here in the mornin'. She has hair about your color and a nice smile. Just tell her that you know Ian and she'll be glad to help—not that she wouldn't anyway." He gave a chuckle. "What time tomorrow, or do ye want to rest a day?"

I shook my head. "I only have a week. Let's say early afternoon, though. I have a feeling I'll be sleeping in."

"Around one?"

"Perfect. And thank you so much."

He doffed his tweed cap and winked before heading out the door.

I faced the young dark-haired man behind the counter. "I have a reservation—Summer McCloud?"

He smiled and handed me the paper to fill out, turning away to answer the telephone.

CHAPTER TEN

I woke to sunlight streaming through my window. I'd left the curtains open the night before, afraid that if they were closed I'd sleep the day away. I grabbed my phone to check the time and then realized that I had a small clock next to my bed. It was nearly nine. Had I missed breakfast? I hoped not because my stomach was rumbling with hunger. I pulled the covers off and hurried to the window, looking out on a beautiful day. In the distance the sea sparkled, pale sand curving before I lost sight of it behind some higher buildings.

I looked forward to buying a pair of cheap mud boots in case there was more bad weather, and hopefully discovering a bit more about the people I was supposed to be researching. And I couldn't wait to explore the beach.

I was still highly confused by the dates, wondering if my Finlay was actually the earlier Finlay who died here in Scotland. But if so, how did he end up in Ames in a grave that didn't belong to him? Ian hadn't even heard of the place.

I dressed hurriedly in wool pants and a sweater, worried about the time between now and Ian's arrival. I had to eat breakfast, and I wanted to shop and take a walk on the beach. I brushed my teeth and pulled my hair up in a messy ponytail. When I looked in the mirror I saw a bright-eyed young woman who had an expression of excitement on her face.

In the dining room downstairs the buffet was still set up. I filled a plate with sausages, eggs, cheese and scones, taking a dollop of the clotted cream, my mouth watering. I poured tea from a carafe and went to find a seat in the nearly empty room. As I was eating the stern woman from the plane arrived, her gaze meeting mine before she moved to the buffet table. How in the world had she ended up in Dornoch at the same hotel? I tried not to stare, concentrating instead on the food on my plate. I gobbled my food and left the dining room, heading to the front desk.

"Where can I find information about the early clans who lived in Sutherland county?" I asked the red-haired woman.

She smiled. "You must be Summer McCloud. Ian called earlier to let me know about you."

I felt a blush rise into my cheeks. "I am. You must be Mairi Flynn. What a lovely hotel you have."

"'Tis been in my family for several generations, although lately it's had a facelift, like the en suite bathrooms."

"I'm sure guests appreciate that."

"They do. Now what was it ye asked? Oh yes, about the clans. There is the wee museum just down the street," she told me. "They have a section with maps and so on to help ye find the historical sites here. Just turn to the left out the door and head down the block."

I thanked her and ran up the stairs to my room to fetch my coat.

It was brisk outside, the air fresh after the rain. Everything had been washed clean, the houses and places of business, crystal clear in the morning sun. The town stretched away, old and new buildings mixing together to create a pleasing panorama of color and style. The sea and beach in the distance beckoned, but first I had to get some information. There would be time later to take a walk. I pulled my hood up and hurried along the street, smiling at various friendly people who walked by me. So far I liked Dornoch very much.

The museum was housed in an old stone building that had seen better days. When I walked inside, I picked up the odor of old musty paper and possibly cigars. I headed to the desk. "Do you have information about Clan McCloud and possibly the Camran family who lived here long ago?"

The gray-haired woman smiled and pointed toward a small room. "The Camrans and Macleods never left, dear, but if yer after early history, ye will find what yer looking for in there."

In the room were the usual artifacts relating to earlier life, with swords and daggers, pots for cooking and hair ornaments and clasps to hold cloaks closed. Bits of cloth from former clothing were laid out in the cases, showing the early weaving techniques and dyes. Small plaques explained what I was looking at.

When I saw the double-edged sword called the claymore, I stopped to take a longer look. *This particular sword was used in the fighting that took place between Clan Macleod and Clan MacKenzie in 1692,* I read. *It was found along the outer walls of Ardvreck Castle in 1918.* I stared at it, a tingle going up both my arms. I wondered if Finlay and Ian's distant relatives had forged it. I moved on, studying other artifacts from the time and reading about ghosts that had been rumored to roam around the ruins.

I hurried back to the front desk. "Do you have more information about the ghosts that haunt Ardvreck Castle?" I asked excitedly.

She looked up, her gray-blue eyes meeting mine. "Funny ye should ask. Not an hour ago another woman was enquiring about the same thing." She reached behind her and pulled out several pamphlets from the cubbies along the wall. "This explains it all. 'Tis too supernatural to be in the regular exhibit, ye ken. But it seems that many have witnessed what is written here."

I took the papers from her, looking down at the various ghost stories listed. "Thank you. What did this other person look like—the one who asked about Ardvreck castle?"

"Older than ye by a good ten years or more—severe lookin' woman with dark hair."

I felt a shiver. "I think she's staying in my hotel."

"Maybe ye should speak with her. She had a book with her about ghosts and how to find them." She smiled before going back to what she'd been doing.

I left the museum and found a coffee shop where I could sit and peruse the papers she'd given me. After my cappuccino came I began to read, surprised by all the stories. According to legend the Macleod's had made a deal with the devil to help them build Ardvreck castle. And in exchange, the devil had asked for the daughter of the clan's chieftain. But before she could be taken, she killed herself by jumping from the tower. Several people who had visited the ruins attested to hearing her crying amongst the walls and tumbled down stones.

I looked up as a young couple walked by, the man dressed in a kilt and high socks. The woman looked normal enough, her dark hair pulled up in a twisted braid on the back of her head. I wondered if there was a festival going on, or if the kilt was normal dress around here.

I gazed down at the pamphlet again, reading another story about the Marquis of Montrose, James Graham. In the spring of 1650 he was held at Ardvreck castle before being transported to Edinburgh for trial and execution. According to the reports, Montrose was a royalist fighting for King Charles against the Covenanters. I had read briefly about this movement at the museum, the covenant signed in 1638 by those opposed to the new liturgy introduced by King Charles I. Many of the populace didn't fancy having a king ruling over them and being their spiritual leader as well. To the covenanters only Jesus Christ could be their spiritual leader. It was a sticking point that turned into a repressive mess, ministers turned out of their churches and preaching in barns and other places, people being arrested for going against their government. If these ministers were caught, they were summarily put to death. The movement ended in 1688 when Prince William of Orange made a bloodless invasion of Great Britain, but the years in between led to many deaths and much hardship.

Montrose was executed in 1650, hung and then drawn and quartered. I shuddered. What a terrible time to be alive. Rumors had it that a tall man dressed in gray had been seen at the castle, assumed to be this Montrose character, although why he would end up there was a mystery to me.

In 1692 Clan Mackenzie attacked and captured the castle, and in 1726 built a classical style dwelling called Calda house, named for the Calda stream close by. But in 1737, Calda house burned to the ground after an all night party that went on into the Sabbath. Everyone was killed. It was assumed that the fire was an act of God, punishment for making merry on the Sabbath, but there were also stories blaming the torching on other members of the Mackenzie clan. Since then various ghosts had been spied around the ruins, as well as a ghostly woman who tourists had seen walking about. I couldn't wait to go.

I looked up at the clock on the wall, surprised to see it was after twelve. It was time to get back to the hotel and meet Ian. I paid at the counter and left the warm cozy shop, excited about what the afternoon might bring.

The wind was gusting off the water, a salt-tinged mist coming with it. I shoved my hands deep in my pockets and bent into it, remembering what Ian had said about if the wind stops…I had to chuckle.

I waited inside the swinging door to the lobby until Ian appeared and hurried out to meet him. I hopped into the car. "Good afternoon," I said brightly. "Can we go to Ardvreck Castle first? I've been reading about all the ghosts hanging around the ruins."

Ian glanced at me, a skeptical look on his face. I wondered if he was worried about the iffy weather after his quip about being stuck in mud in the middle of nowhere. But he agreed, even if there was little enthusiasm in his tone. He pulled away from the curb and headed slowly through town.

"I may as well tell you why I'm here," I chattered on. "I'm trying to find a murderer."

"A murderer? And ye ken this murderer might be hangin' about a centuries old ruin?"

"The murderer died long ago…"

"Doin' some research on your ancestors, then?"

"Something like that."

"Ye need to meet the local loony, Owen Mackenzie. He's a ghost whisperer."

"Owen talks with ghosts?"

"Aye, so he says. But ye canna prove it by me."

A Mackenzie, the other name Finlay had mentioned, and also the clan who had taken Ardvreck castle from Clan Macleod. "I would like to meet him."

Ian's eyes lit up. "How about tonight at my house for dinner? Owen is always up for a free meal."

"Can he make it on such short notice?"

"I'll call him on my cell. I'll fix it for tonight around seven." He glanced at me with a sly grin. "That is if ye haven't given me cause to get a tow truck by then."

"Are we heading into some wild place where we might fall into a bog or a sink hole?"

Ian chuckled. "Ye'd be surprised, lass. Ask that question after we've been to Ardvreck Castle. And who knows where ye'll want me to take ye to tomorrow? Settlements are few and far between up north."

"There is the Calda house."

"That we can see today—'tis nae far from the castle ruins."

"Tomorrow…maybe an ancient graveyard or two?"

"That I can do. There are several close to Dornoch."

"With McCloud on the gravestones?"

He shrugged. "Havna spent much time there, I confess. Ye can ask Owen."

It took us an hour and a half to reach the bare hills around Loch Assynt. It was beautiful and wild, with hawks soaring above us, a herd of red deer on the small mountain close to the ruin. Clouds raced above us, wild horses with their tails flying, pale blue sky leading them on.

The ruin stood on a rocky promontory overlooking the lake—a perfect spot for defensive purposes. A larger mountain rose on the other side, its rounded top covered with snow. The water lay like a mirror, the dull reddish-green hills reflected in its pristine surface. The barrenness of the place gave me a fluttery feeling in my belly, as though I recognized it somehow. I imagined walking barefoot across the landscape with a basket over my arm to gather heather and herbs. Had I lived here once? After all, I was a McCloud—my ancestors must be buried around here somewhere.

Ian pulled the car off the dirt track and cut the motor. "If ye dinna mind I'll wait here out of the cold."

"That's fine," I said, stepping out of the car. As soon as I began to climb the hill the wind came up, sending bits of grass and tiny sand particles flying. I pulled up my hood and bent into it. When I reached the crumbling stone edifice I stopped to take a look around, my gaze pulled to the ruffled surface of the lake that had been so placid when we arrived. When I heard voices I peeked around a wall, surprised to see the very same woman who'd sat beside me on the flight to London. With her was an older man, the two of them bent to her book on ghosts. I stayed where I was until I heard their voices fading.

As soon as I was sure they were gone I stepped around the tower to enter what had been the castle interior, surprised to see a young woman sitting on a tumbled rock. She was wearing a belted shift with frayed edges, long dark hair covering her face. She was crying. When I stepped out she looked up, her eyes widening. "Aren't you cold?" I asked, pointing to her bare feet, her exposed neck, and the lightweight dress.

She said something in a brogue I couldn't understand at all. Could that really be English? "What are you doing here?" I asked, moving closer.

Her gaze went to the lake before she turned back, her wide gray eyes filled with tears. "Me wee bairn, he is gain."

"Bairn—what--?"

But before she could answer she began to fade, and a second later she had disappeared altogether. A ghost. I wondered if she was the one mentioned in the papers the woman at the museum had given me. If so, she could be a Macleod. I wanted to ask her some questions, but how to coax her back?

I was wandering through the rest of the ruins, hoping to catch sight of her, or maybe another ghost or two, when a sudden gloom came over. When I looked up, a blanket of dark clouds had concealed the sun. A moment later my attention was taken to the hillside, as a group of shadowy soldiers brandishing swords ran helter skelter down its rough, grass-tufted sides. A momentary chill went down my arms as I registered how much death had happened here. When a raindrop landed on my face I decided it was time to go.

By the time I was halfway to the car the sky opened up, thunder rumbling in the distance. I ran, slipping in mud as I hurtled toward the car. When I reached it Ian already had the door open, a newspaper held over his head. Once I climbed inside he hurried around to get in behind the wheel. "You weren't kidding about changes in weather," I said, shaking out my hood and settling back. "Did you see the woman and man who were up there?"

Ian shook his head. "Must have had me head in the newspaper."

"Did you see or hear a car?"

"Nae, but they may have walked a good distance to get here. There is a car park over by Calda House."

"I think I saw a ghost," I said, testing him. "She was in the ruins and dressed in an outfit that was anything but modern. I think I saw a dress just like it in the museum What does the word bairn mean?"

"Bairn—'tis a child."

"She said her bairn was gone."

Ian stared out the windshield watching the rain course down the glass. "Maybe she was part of the massacre that took place here early on."

"You mean when Clan Mackenzie took over?"

"They drove out Clan Macleod. Possibly her bairn was killed in the fracas."

"I saw some soldier's too. They were running down the hill holding these enormous swords."

"Ye must have witnessed the battle, lass—at least a moment of it."

There was a lonesome sadness here that I'd picked up during my time in and around the ruins. 'Lonely stretch' was how Ian had described it. And it was. "It's too wet now to visit Calda house. Would you mind driving me up another day?"

"'Tis your choice, lass."

It was clear that Ian didn't much like it up here. We backed out, tires whirring for a moment as we encountered the silt-like mud, but a moment later we found traction and moved along the dirt track toward the tarmac. I heard his sigh of relief.

"Did you reach your friend?" I asked once we were heading along the main road.

"I did. Owen is anxious to meet ye."

I wondered about Owen and the description of him. "Why do you call him the local loony?"

Ian chuckled. "Ye will ken when ye meet him."

The sun had come out again by the time we reached the Inn. "I'll be back to get ye a little before seven. Ye best take a rest before that, lassie. Ye look done in."

I did? "See you later, then. And thanks so much for today."

In my room I examined my face in the mirror. My eyes looked hollow, with dark smudges beneath them. I needed a shower and I had to call home before I headed out again. So much for a walk on the beach.

I sat on the bed and tried to calculate what time it was at home, finally deciding that if it was six in the evening here, it was late morning there. I dialed the number, surprised when the call went through.

"Summer!" Agnes cried. "How is it going?"

"It's cold and rainy, but still amazing. Funny thing about my Finlay—I think he might be in the wrong grave."

"Wrong grave? What are you talking about?"

"I think it's his son in that grave. My Finlay must be his father. You see…"

"So tell me about Scotland—your hotel—what did you do today? What's the weather like besides rainy?"

"The hotel is perfect, and I have a driver who took me to a castle ruin today. I talked to a ghost."

"You didn't!"

"I did. And the weird thing is, I think she was a McCloud."

"Wow, Summer!"

"How are you? How's the store?"

"Everything's going fine, although I don't know how you put up with your customers. They spend hours here and then don't buy anything."

"I know," I laughed. "But they're my regulars. Have you seen Becky? I wonder how the animals are doing."

"She came in this morning—said everything is fine at your house. Told me to ask you to look up Henderson."

"I doubt I'll have time, but maybe. I'm meeting a man tonight who supposedly talks to ghosts."

"Ah, a kindred spirit, so to speak."

"That's funny, Agnes. He's been described to me as loony. It should be interesting."

"Who says that?"

"My driver who knows him. I'm going to his house tonight for dinner to meet Owen, the loony."

"Sounds like you're having a good time."

"Have you—did you—?"

"If you're going to ask about Jerry, don't bother. I haven't heard a word."

"It's funny, I haven't thought about him at all."

"Well, don't. It's not worth the bother, especially when you're having an adventure. Call me in a couple of days, okay?"

"I will. And thanks for taking such good care of Tarot and Tea. And if you see Becky, thank her too."

"I will. Take care and have fun. Talk to you soon."

When I hung up, Jerry loomed into my headspace. *Go away,* I said.

I dressed in a black wool skirt and hip length red sweater, pulling on the Frye boots I'd brought along. I pulled my hair back and secured it with a silver clip before adding eyeliner to my tired looking gray-green eyes. After that I filled in my lips with a pale pinkish color to take away my pallor.

I was waiting by the door when Ian drove up, his smile making me less nervous about what was to come. It wasn't every day I got to meet another person who could talk to ghosts. "I'm sorry I don't have a bottle of wine to contribute," I said, slipping in beside him.

"Dinna worry, lass. We have plenty of wine. Catriona, my lady friend, is especially fond of the fermented grape and has good taste. I hope ye eat meat—she's prepared shepherd's pie."

"One of my favorites. I'm starving."

He pulled away from the curb and headed along the rain-drenched street. The rain had been coming down in buckets for the past half hour. It was hard to know how to dress here.

"Owen wasn't at the house when I left, but I expect he'll be there when we get back."

I felt a frisson of nerves. "How old is Owen?"

"Hmm—hard to say. I expect he'll be around your age, maybe a bit older."

Around my age? I'd pictured a man of fifty. Now I

10

felt really nervous. "Is he married?"

"Ach, no, lass. Owen is a free spirit—can't be held down for longer than a day before he breaks free."

"What does he do?"

"A little of this, a little of that. Sort of a jack of all trades, I suppose," he added vaguely.

I gazed at the orange glow of streetlights reflected in the rain puddles, the mist rising from the tarmac. "How long will the rains last?"

"They're predictin' dry weather tomorrow."

"Oh good. I want to take another look up there at Calda House."

"I may not be able to drive ye tomorrow. My lady has an appointment. But maybe Owen will take ye, if ye get on, that is."

"But you said you were free all week."

Ian looked abashed for a moment. "This came up suddenly. I am sorry, lass."

"It's okay—sorry," I said quickly, realizing that something health related was happening with Catriona.

The rest of the short trip was made in uncomfortable silence. We pulled up in front of a small brick house with a walled garden in front. I could see that in good weather there would be bushes and flowers blooming, but at this time of year there was nothing but mud and bare branches. The front door held a wreath of holly with a bright red ribbon, reminding me that Christmas was just around the corner.

CHAPTER ELEVEN

As soon as I walked through Ian's door and saw Catriona standing there I felt at home. She was rosy-cheeked with crow's feet around her wide eyes, her smile of welcome taking away my worries. She came forward to greet me in the European way, a kiss on both cheeks. Once we said hello I looked around the living room, noting the fire burning brightly, the tray of cheese and other delights on the coffee table in front of the worn, but comfortable looking, couch. Several landscapes hung on the walls, adding to the homey feeling.

I was about to pick up a cracker and some cheese when a man entered the living room from the kitchen. He was tall and broad-shouldered, wearing loose brown corduroys and a hand-knit sweater in browns and grays. Long chestnut hair lay tangled around his angular face, as though he hadn't bothered to comb it. Vivid blue eyes met mine, his gaze intense. My face was suddenly hot, my throat going dry as his unabashed stare bored a hole into my psyche.

"Summer, this is Owen, the man I spoke to you about."

I opened my mouth but nothing came out as he moved toward me, his hand extended. I put my hand in his, feeling a tingle move up my arm and settle somewhere in my heart region. He was handsome and striking, a man I could imagine wearing a kilt and running across the moors with a broadsword in his hand.

"Guid to meet ye," he said in a stronger brogue than I'd heard since my ghost at the castle.

I nodded, as yet unable to form words. My awkwardness eased when Catriona came by to hand me a goblet of wine. I took it from her, realizing that my hand was shaking. "Thank you," I said, using my other hand to steady the glass and keep the red wine from spilling over the edge.

"Come sit," she said, patting the couch next to where she lowered herself. "Ian will put the finishing touches on the food, won't ye love?" she asked with a sly glance and smile at Ian.

"For you, anything," he said, taking himself off to the kitchen.

In the meantime Owen had seated himself in a chair next to the couch, a glass of wine held securely in his large hand. "Ye fancy ghosts?" he asked me, leaning forward.

There was something of the uncanny about the man. He almost seemed like he came from some distant time when men fought with each other over sheep and land, the brawls ending in one or both of them dead. "Like them? I guess you could say that. I can talk to them sometimes," I managed to mumble, afraid to see what expression Catriona might have on her face.

He chuckled. "'Tis the same for me. We were

destined to meet."

He took a sip of wine, his eyebrows rising as our eyes met over his glass.

"I—I came to find out about--"

"I ken the reason for yer visit. Ian told me all about it, includin' what happened up at Ardvreck just this very day."

I turned to Catriona who was watching me expectantly. "I saw a woman who had to be a ghost. She told me she'd lost her bairn. Ian thinks she was…"

"A Macleod for sure," Owen supplied. "The ghost who haunts those two ruins. I've had several conversations with the woman. Her name was Brigid."

"You know her? She disappeared before I could ask her anything."

He nodded, his eyes never leaving my face. "I can take ye back up there while Ian is…" He turned to Catriona.

"While Ian is taking me to a doctor's appointment," she finished matter-of-factly. "Nothing too worrisome—only women's problems."

She smiled but I detected a hint of worry. "I'd like that," I answered, but in truth the idea of being alone with the man did something to my insides. He was too good-looking, and too…I wasn't sure what it was about him, only that I'd never felt this kind of attraction in such a visceral way, especially on just meeting someone. And there was also that ethereal aspect of him that I found unsettling.

"Tomorrow?"

I tried to come up with some excuse for why not, but in the end I only nodded.

The rest of the evening went by in a blur of good food, too much wine, and trying to avoid Owen's intense gaze. It was late when I finally decided it was time to get to bed. Jet lag had taken over and I was barely able to carry on a rational conversation. Had I really been in Scotland for only two days? It seemed like a lifetime. "I have to go," I said bluntly, standing.

Owen immediately jumped up. "I'll drive ye back."

I glanced at Ian who nodded. He did look tired. "Okay," I said, knowing that declining the offer would be rude.

Ian fetched my coat from the hall closet and handed it over. "Hope you enjoy tomorrow," he whispered, winking.

"I hope so too," I muttered. "Thank you, Catriona!" I called before heading toward the door Owen held open.

"Please come again, dearie," she called back.

I followed Owen out the door and waited while he opened the car door for me. When he slipped behind the wheel he glanced over. "I knew ye were comin' lass. I've been waitin' for ye."

A frisson of nervousness went down my spine. I tried to smile but I was sure it ended up looking like a grimace. "How could you know? I hardly knew myself until a couple of weeks ago."

"I'm the local loony, remember? I have an uncanny sense sometimes." He turned the key and the car roared to life.

"You can tell the future…are you clairvoyant?"

He laughed. "I am a Mackenzie and ye are a Macleod. We are old friends."

I turned to stare at his profile as we headed onto the main road. "Two warring clans? How could we be old friends?"

He smiled and slanted a glance my way before turning back to the wet road. "Two clans that intermingled, lass. There was much intermarriage between 'em."

"Really? I thought they hated each other."

"Without intermarriage the clans would become impure—'twas done for the gene pool. For instance, you and I could have married and had children together."

A very strange sensation moved in my belly. "And the offspring would be Mackenzies."

"Aye, they were."

My head jerked around to stare at him. "What do you mean, 'they were'?"

"Oh, sorry. I meant to say, they would have been."

But I had the distinct impression that he'd meant what he'd said. "Are you saying we may be related?"

He let out a low laugh. "Nae. I'd be much more inclined to say we've been lovers in the distant past."

This time I kept my eyes forward, shocked into silence. The way he'd said those words made me uncomfortable, and more than a little nervous. How in the world would I manage an entire day with this man? He could be a rapist or a murderer, for all I knew. But then I thought of Ian and Catriona. A friend of theirs had to be okay.

When we arrived in front of the Dornoch Inn I breathed a sigh of relief.

I opened my door. "Thanks for the ride, Owen."

"What time tomorrow?"

I opened my mouth and closed it. Could I beg off? But the look in those indigo eyes of his forced me to come up with an answer. I was only here for a few days, and Calda house was important to my mission. "Around ten?"

He nodded and waited until I closed my door before pulling away from the curb.

I stood there in the pouring rain until his taillights moved into the darkness, my heart beating a little faster than it should.

I woke from the cold. The fire in the fireplace had gone out and the quilt wasn't doing the job. I rose from the bed to look out the tiny window, noticing silvery flakes falling from a dark dark sky. 'Twas late for snow, the early grasses already poking up their tiny heads. I hoped the cold wouldn't stop their upward growth. In the cold distance I could see the dark shapes of trees, the forest where the deer and other game lived.

My hand went to my belly where new life burgeoned. The bairn would be born when the heather bloomed again. I was suddenly aware of the cold stone under my bare feet and hurried back to the bed. When I climbed beneath the covers an arm pulled me close. "Are ye daft? 'Tis no time to be traipsin' about--shall I build up the fire again?"

I stared into the dark blue liquid eyes of my man, love welling inside me. "Nae, 'tis nearly the morn."

"T'will only take a wee meenit," he said, swinging his long legs free of our warm nest.

I watched him move to the fireplace to throw more peat on the still glowing coals, his muslin nightshirt hanging loose as he crouched. The temperature had dropped without him next to me. "Make haste, Owen," I said, curling into myself to stop the shivering. A flame lit up his face for an instant, showing the soft hairs on his chin, the shadows of his cheekbones, the curve of hair falling forward as he bent to the fire. I never grew tired of looking at him.

When he headed back to the bed he grabbed my long braid and pulled me to him. I felt his steady heartbeat, reveling in the warmth that always radiated from his body, as though he had his own fire burning deep within his body. "I'll warm ye up," he whispered.

I shivered, lifting my face to meet his mouth. This time my trembling had nothing to do with the cold. When he pushed me back and stretched against me I forgot about the cold, forgot about everything but my love for him and this precious moment in time. Too soon he would be away again, leaving me to worry until he returned.

I woke with a sudden intake of breath, my pulse pounding in my ears. That was like no dream I'd ever had—it seemed more like a vision from some distant past when Owen and I were together. How could that be? I sat up in bed and pulled my knees in, trying to slow the pounding in my chest and make sense of what was still rolling though my body. I had to look down to make sure

I wasn't pregnant—it was that real.

I stumbled from the bed, my head fuzzy and still back in that time. The terrain was different, covered in heavy forests. What period in history was it? The saffron nightshirt Owen wore was simple---maybe linen? And I thought I might have been wearing the same sort of shirt, remembering the lightness of the fabric when he pushed it up...my face turned hot at the vivid memory of what happened next.

I tried to remember the landscape outside the window. Were we in what had been Ardvreck Castle? I vaguely remembered the sheen of water in the distance, the dark of trees. The snow and the stormy night sky had obliterated a further view. And there was something...a fear at the back of my mind as we coupled, a feeling that I had to grab happiness whenever I could—as though something terrible might take Owen from me at any moment. Was this early enough to be related to the invasion of England in the year 1296, or was this possibly still about the feud between Clan Macleod and Clan Mackenzie in the late 1600's? Who was I in this scenario? And who was the baby I carried...

After taking a quick shower I went down to breakfast, my head filled with the 'dream'. When Mairi said hello I started, brought back from my meanderings, her warm smile a comfort. "Good morning, Mairi. Can I ask you a question?"

"Of course," she said, pausing next to where I was seated.

"What did men and women in the seventeen hundreds wear to bed?"

She let out a soft chuckle. "I suspect it was the shift of linen, although I am no historian. Why do ye ask?"

I gazed into her green eyes, surprised by the perceptive look in them. "I had a most peculiar dream," I answered, trying to hide the blush that crept up my neck.

She smiled. "Seems to be the way of things here," she said. "Many of my guests have these sorts of vivid dreams that they can nae explain. I tell them that they must have lived here in some past life—this hotel dates back to the 1600's. Perhaps that explains it?"

"The dream took place in a stone building—possibly Ardvreck castle."

"Aye. Yer last name is Macleod, is it not?"

"Yes."

She raised her eyebrows and shrugged and left me to my musings. I drank my tea and let my mind wander. But before I got to the bottom of my cup I realized that in fifteen short minutes Owen would be arriving to pick me up. Nerves shredded whatever calm I had, the thought of the day giving me palpitations. But I didn't have a number to call to cancel the day's activities. And I had to admit that part of me was very much looking forward to seeing him again.

CHAPTER TWELVE

I waited outside in bright sunlight, trying hard to regulate my breathing. *It will be fine*, I told myself. *It was only a dream, only a dream.* But I knew that wasn't the truth. I had no control over whatever was going on, nor did I know where it came from.

Owen rolled up to the curb in Ian's car and left it idling. A second later he was out and holding the door open for me. He was dressed in the same cords and heavy sweater, work boots on his feet. I tried to avoid looking at him as I slid into the front seat, willing my breathing back to normal.

"Are ye quite well, lass?"

As soon as our eyes met my face grew hot. "I'm fine," I lied, trying not to remember the way he'd looked at me the night before in my 'dream', or the feel of that mouth on mine.

"Ye dinna look fine. Are ye sure ye wish to be in my company?"

"Yes, I'm sure. I want to see Calda house today—do you mind driving up there?"

"'Twould please me greatly," he smiled, putting the car into gear.

I asked him about the weather and if he knew what

was happening with Catriona as we drove along the narrow road leading to the castle ruins.

"Catriona has had some unusual bleedin'," he answered, keeping his eyes on the road.

That didn't sound good. "How long have you known them?"

He let out a chortle. "Do ye want the truth?"

"Of course I do," I said, irritated.

"Would ye believe centuries?"

I thought of my dream. "No, I wouldn't."

"Well then, let's just say we've known each other for quite a while."

"Why does Ian call you the local loony?"

He let out a musical laugh that filled the small car. "He likes to make light of what I am, I suppose."

"What you are—like talking to ghosts?"

"That and other things."

I didn't ask what other things. His body next to mine felt like a magnet that was pulling me closer and closer. Thank goodness it was only happening on a psychic level.

When we reached the loch he drove the car off the road close to the ruin of Calda house and cut the engine. The landscape was the same as the day before, but this time the sun shone down on the lake, and a hazy mist rose from the water. We weren't far from the castle ruins. I scanned what was left of the walls of Calda house. It was impressive. "The place was enormous."

"Aye, and drafty."

"Are you telling me you lived there in a past life?"

He scoffed. "Would ye believe me if I did?"

I shrugged and opened my door, getting out before he could hurry around the car. He was right beside me when I headed toward the ruin, the sound of his breathing making me very aware of how close our bodies were to each other. Something caught my eye and I turned to see a man that looked surprisingly like Finlay stealthily approaching Calda house. I grabbed Owen's arm. "Who is that?"

"That is Finlay Ross Macleod comin' to take ye away from me."

I swung my gaze to his. "What?"

His eyes narrowed in amusement. "'Tis why yer here, lass—to find out what happened so many years ago."

I stared into his indigo eyes. "You know why I'm here? How?"

He raised his eyebrows for a second and gave a one-shoulder shrug, his hands splayed.

"I—I had a dream last night," I blurted before I could stop myself.

"A disturbin' dream, was it?"

"You could say that. You were in it."

"Did I hurt ye?"

When I gazed at him, his liquid eyes were troubled. I wanted to kiss him in the worst way. "No, nothing like that—we—I think we were married."

He smiled. "Ye remembered."

"Remembered what? It was only a dream."

"Were ye with child?"

"Well, yes. But what does that have to do with it?"

He nodded and stared at the hills in the distance. "We were together before the Jacobite rebellion of 1715—'twas James the second who should have been on the throne." He turned to meet my bewildered gaze. "Our bairn was a lassie that time around. The next one, in 1720, was a laddie."

"That wasn't me!" I shouted.

He reached to take my hand. "Calm yerself, lass. Ian told me ye spoke with a ghost. Is this nae true?"

"Yes, but this isn't about ghosts, this is...I don't know what this is!"

He pulled me to him. "'Tis a lot to take in all at once," he said, his warm breath on my neck. "Have ye never seen yer past lives?"

I shook my head, pulling away and trying to wipe my eyes. "I talk to ghosts, but I..."

"Ye've nae had a vision like the one of us together."

I met his concerned gaze. "That's right. How do you know all this, anyway?"

"I recognized ye the moment I laid eyes on ye, lass. Did ye nae wonder why I stared so?"

"I did wonder, especially since I—you—you—" I stopped myself, not sure what to say.

"Ye loved me once."

"What happened to us? What happened to our children?"

"The man ye just saw, Finlay Macleod, claimed all three of ye. I swore I'd get even with the man, and I did."

"Claimed me. Do you mean Finlay was my father?"

"The Macleods and the Mackenzies were bitter

enemies. Finlay had his reasons for what he did. He was your great-uncle and he dinna wish ye to be with a Mackenzie."

"You killed Finlay in your past life?" I whispered, staring at him. He didn't answer, his gaze staying on mine so long I had to look away. "Did you stab him in the back?"

"He was runnin' from me like the coward he was, and I caught up to him. I cut his head off with a claymore." His jaw clenched. "'Twas a fittin' end."

A past memory or vision arrived unbidden in my mind. I felt the emotional pain of being taken from the man I loved, kept from him by Finlay's threats to hurt my children if I tried to escape. Finlay had said that no Mackenzie could take what was rightfully his. But in my heart I knew he wanted me to make the fires and do the cooking and the washing, fetch the water, gather the herbs and greens, and do the milking. He worked me hard, and when I got sick he didn't fetch the healer. He was a cruel man.

A wave of sickness took my breath away and I doubled over, my hands on my stomach. I could *feel* the spasms and the vomiting, the darkness that took me. I remembered the fear and sorrow registered on my two children's sweet faces as I left the world. I died without seeing Owen, without being able to say goodbye. I was crying now, bent over with the memories.

Owen grabbed my arm. "What is it, lass? Are ye quite all right?"

"No," I gasped. I looked up at him. "I saw it, Owen.

I felt the pain of being separated from you. I felt my death. It was terrible."

"Ah, lassie. I am sorry. I never meant to hurt ye so."

"You didn't hurt me—it was Finlay. But...I'm still so confused. He told me he had a wife, Elsbeth, but she wasn't there in my vision."

"Elsbeth left him, went off on her own. "Tis why he was determined to take ye from me."

"He didn't tell me that part," I muttered, staring into the distance. "Finlay asked me to come here to find out who murdered him. He's hanging around his son's grave back in Ames, Connecticut."

Owen looked surprised. "Nae sure how his ghost ended up there. I killed him here. Some Macleod collected his body, as I recall. And the man knew exactly who was comin' after him."

"Why did Elsbeth leave him?"

"'The man abused her until she had enough. Her Da collected her and the bairns one day, and 'twas the end of it." Owen scowled, staring into the distance.

"You knew her?"

He swung his gaze back. "I was a wee laddie. She was nae the same after her marriage."

I thought of the Finlay in the graveyard. This didn't sound like the same man. According to the way Finlay talked, Elsbeth was the love of his life. But the vision I'd just had was very real. Maybe he didn't remember his cruelty. He certainly seemed vague on several other issues, even the date of his death.

My gaze went to Calda house, Ardvreck castle ruin in

the distance. For a moment I saw the two buildings as they'd been, majestic and imposing. I felt angry with the injustice of it all, even knowing that it all happened long ago. "You had good reason for killing him," I said, meeting Owen's clear gaze.

His jaw unclenched, his eyes going soft. "I did."

And before I knew what was happening he'd pulled me into his arms and was kissing me. Instead of pushing him away, I melted, my consciousness going to that past me who had loved him and had two babies with him, all the pain of being separated rising up as I kissed him back. When he finally released me we stood staring at one another, neither of us able to utter a word.

"I love ye, lass," he whispered a moment later. "I never stopped."

"But that was centuries ago, Owen. I'm not that person now, and neither are you."

"And who was it just kissed me?"

"I—I don't know."

He took hold of my hand. "I'll show ye the ruin and then we can find a quiet spot where—"

"Where you can take advantage of me?"

"Why would ye say that? Ye dinna trust me?"

I let out a sigh. "I don't know what's happening here…I only know that I feel…"

"Dinna fash, lass." He went ahead, leading the way into the center of Calda house.

I followed him.

The two of us stood on the grass in the center of the ruin. I closed my eyes, picturing the opulence, the trappings of wealth, and the many rooms the house had once had. There had been several fireplaces. I could see feel the warmth that radiated from them. But away from the fires the rooms were bitter cold.

This was where I'd been in my first vision. This was the place where Finlay had found me. It happened when Owen was away and the rest of the clan had gone to the traveling markets that came by every month or so. I heard the screams of my two babies as he dragged the three of us away. "We lived here," I said quietly, looking over at Owen.

"Aye. We had a guid room. 'Tis where Annie was born. The house burned down in 1737."

"Annie? That was our baby's name?"

He nodded. "And Ross was the laddie born a few years later."

"What happened to me once you killed Finlay?"

His eyes clouded. "Ye were already gone to your death, lass. 'Twas why I vowed to murder the man who put ye in harm's way. Because of him I had too few years with ye."

Tears came into my eyes again as I listened to him. Ours had been a tragic love story. "What did I die of? What happened to our children?"

"Ye caught the fever that took down so many during the time. Ye were weak from how hard ye worked, the cold of that particular winter. Our bairns survived and went on. 'Tis why ye are here now."

I let out a long sigh and wiped my eyes. When he took hold of my hand I let him lead me away like a child.

I felt drained and sad, the past like a heavy weight on my chest. Once we were in the car he drove off in another direction. "Where are we going?"

"There is a spot up here where we can talk over a cup o' tea."

I pictured a small wayside Inn with a fire burning merrily, the smell of scones. I settled back and closed my eyes, trying not to see him in his nightshirt in front of the fire, muscles taut and visible through the light fabric.

I was dozing when I felt the car roll to a stop. I opened my eyes, surprised to see a small stone house nestled into the side of a hill. "What's this?"

"'Tis a remnant of what was once mine." He opened his door and stepped out, meeting me in front of the car. When he took my hand I let him pull me toward a heavy wooden door hanging by one hinge. He pushed the door aside with his boot to enter the dark space. I stood in the doorway trying to adjust to the darkness. There was a heavy feeling here, as though past energy had gathered and remained. A moment later he'd lit a couple of candles and was bent to the cold fireplace.

My first thought was, ugh, it smells like mouse droppings and damp, but once the candles were lit I noticed a gleaming Welsh dresser against one wall, and in front of the fireplace, wooden chairs hugged a rough-hewn table set with pewter dishes and goblets. On the far wall was a bed, a bright quilt covering the thick mattress. Threadbare rugs lay across the dirt floors, their once vivid colors faded. For a moment I smelled baking bread, and heard the hiss of a teakettle, the sound of distant voices.

I moved next to where he poked at the fire, holding my cold fingers out to warm them. There was no wood on the grate, but I recognized the peat as though I'd seen it a million times. Wood was too precious a commodity to burn. "Do you live here?"

"Sometimes I come here. 'Twas in my family, ye ken, long ago."

"Where's our tea?" I asked, laughing. There didn't seem to be much in the way of food.

"I can make ye a cup if ye can wait while I fetch water. There's an old well out back."

I took hold of his arm as he turned. "Don't bother."

Our eyes met and locked and a second later he lifted me in his arms and carried me back to the bed. I wanted to protest, but it was as though I'd become this other woman—the one who'd loved this man. My pulse quickened as he pulled off his sweater and removed his corduroys.

"Is this all right with ye, lass?" he whispered once all our clothes had been discarded on the floor next to the bed. His eyes held mine, dark with longing.

I nodded and reached for him, my mind on our past and what I felt. He was my husband, my lover, and the father of my children. "What was my name?"

He smiled and whispered, "'Twas Aine."

"Do I look like her?"

"Aye, lass. Ye do." When he bent to kiss me I was lost in the dream of us as we had been before, my hunger for him taking away any hesitation. Our tears mingled as we moved together, and when it was over we fell asleep wrapped in each other's arms.

When I woke it was growing dark. Owen was by the fire, throwing more peat on the coals, his crouched form similar to my vision of him. But now I could clearly see his back, the scars that crisscrossed the muscle. A teakettle hung on an iron pole and I smelled meat cooking.

I pulled on my long sweater and went to kneel next to him. "What are you doing?"

"I'm making us some dinner," he said, meeting my gaze. "I snared a rabbit and skinned it while ye were sleeping."

How long had I been asleep? I gazed at his naked body, picturing him running through the heather in the cold. The rabbit was roasting on an open iron skillet that rested on a grate. "It smells good. Wish we had some vegetables to go with it." I traced his scars with my fingers. "How did you get these?"

"Torture, lass. Punishment for bein' a Mackenzie."

"But you aren't the man from the past."

He smiled. "I am that man, the same as I was the day we married. As far as vegetables, there are none this time o' year."

I thought about all the vegetables in the market. Time of year had nothing to do with it. I let his other statement go by, certain he was being poetic. "The meat will be enough," I said, moving to the bed to pull on my jeans. "Aren't you cold?"

"I dinna feel the cold." I watched him flip the meat with a pronged tool, his actions sure. "Will ye stay here with me tonight?" he asked without turning.

"I suppose so—there isn't any reason I need to go back." I glanced at the window that revealed a square of darkness. The door next to it was now closed and sound. "And anyway, it's late. Driving back seems silly."

"Aye."

A few minutes later he cut the meat off the bones, dividing it between us. "I have some ale if ye'd like," he said, producing a crock. He poured liquid into the pewter goblets.

"Was all this in your family?" I asked, gesturing to the furniture, the bed, the rugs and the table settings.

"Aye. 'Tis all I have left of that time. Mo ghra thu," he said, lifting the cup to his lips.

"Is that Gaelic? What does it mean?"

He smiled. "Ye are my love," he translated.

I took a tiny sip, surprised to find it smooth and tasty. "To us," I said, lifting my cup again. I looked around the candle-lit room, wondering where the ale had come from. And the rabbit…

"Tell me more about our past life," I asked later after we'd finished eating and were sitting next to each other in front of the fire.

"We lived simply. Ye took care of the bairns, gathered the greens and made the bannock, while I rode out with the rest o' the lads, into the forest to hunt and stave off the raiders. I always hated leavin' ye. I must have known what was comin'."

"You mean Finlay."

"Aye. The man was always lurkin' in the back of my

mind like a plague. He'd threatened to take ye several times before he finally made his move. We'd fought over it. There were other dangers as well, what with warrin' clans sneakin' about. 'Twas no time for a woman alone."

I thought of the Finlay I knew—handsome, funny and seemingly kind. "Finlay seems nice now," I said.

Owen frowned, staring into the fire. "He's had a lot o' years to think about his actions. Maybe he regrets what he did. 'Twas his ghost who sent ye here—is that right?"

I nodded. "Maybe he wanted us to meet, although how he would know you were alive in this timeline is a mystery to me."

Owen rose from his place next to me, his jaw clenching. "Ye came for me, lass—to meet me, to be with me."

He paced like a caged animal, his eyes turning stormy. He scared me for a moment, intense energy coming off him in waves. And I thought Jerry's anger was bad? I would not want this man's rage directed at me. "What's wrong, Owen?"

Several warring emotions crossed his features. "'Tis nothin', only my strong affection for ye."

I let out a breath. "I feel the same way."

He moved next to me again, folding his long legs under him. I put my hand on his thigh.

He gazed at me. "I will miss ye," he whispered.

"I'm not going anywhere—oh, you mean when I go back home. Maybe you can fly to the States." I watched him, trying to picture this wild man on the streets of Ames.

He scoffed and watched the flames, running his fingers through his tangled hair.

"Why not?"

His smile was sad. "Because I am stuck here, lass."

"You don't have to be. If it's money you're worried about maybe I can get my—"

He put his finger on my mouth and then leaned in to kiss me. I kissed him back, caught up in his heat and the surge of emotion that made me nearly delirious with desire.

Once we'd moved to the bed he took his time, lingering over my body as though memorizing every inch of it. Tears flowed from his eyes as we became one, his whispered words of Gaelic like memories of a distant dream. The past and present wove together in my mind as I slipped from one to the other.

I saw myself as I'd been back then, a different person with different worries, a baby coming and what that meant for me and for us: possible problems with the birth, illness--mine or the baby's, or both, threatening weather, lack of food—all these things were on my mind back then. I worried that he'd be gone too long, or that he'd be killed when he was away, afraid of the warring clans and what I faced being alone, frightened about disease claiming one or all of us. In this past world I desperately needed him. Without a man I wouldn't survive. But along with this awareness, I was here now, a different person and yet the same.

We spent most of the night awake, him whispering words I didn't understand, and me kissing his ear, his neck, his mouth, my hand flat on his chest to feel his heart beat. His fingers were buried in my hair as we coupled, his eyes never leaving mine, until he bent to place his mouth on mine. He seemed unable to get enough of me, a sort of desperation in his eyes as we made love again and again. I finally fell asleep with my head resting against his shoulder, his arm holding me solidly against him.

I woke sometime later feeling cold. Owen was not in the bed and the fire was out. I rose and found my clothes, dressing quickly. The window revealed a gray dawn sky, and when I glanced back at the bed, the quilt was no longer bright. I examined it more closely, surprised to see that it was full of moth holes and stiff with age. Underneath it was a straw mattress that I was sure had been filled with down the night before.

The furniture and rugs were all gone, leaving a cold dirt floor covered in mouse droppings, grass and dried leaves. The fireplace looked unused, with cobwebs wound inside the chimney. No remnants of our dinner remained. I stared around blankly, wondering how this could be. Had we been in some Fae world the night before—some magical place?

When I pushed the door open, it swung out, creaking as it leaned precariously on its one hinge. I stumbled outside, glad to see the car still parked where it had been. At least Owen hadn't driven away and left me here. But where was he?

"Owen!" I shouted. I walked a good half a mile in a widening circle, calling for him until my throat went hoarse. I even headed up the hill in back of the cottage, wondering if he'd decided to take a walk. But there were no footprints in the mud, and when I called I got no answer. The clouds were massing again and it looked like rain was imminent.

I drove the car to Ardvreck castle ruin and Calda house to see if he was there—maybe he'd taken a longer walk than I thought. But when I got there and called his name, the place was as silent as a tomb. I had a pang of loneliness, as though part of me had disappeared with Owen, and then panic raced through me as I registered his absence. But I wasn't that past woman. I lived in this time when women were independent and self-sufficient. I didn't need him to take care of me. But the feeling remained.

I wandered around aimlessly looking for him, climbing down into crevasses that led to boggy areas where tracks of animals had been left in the mud. This entire area was a 'lonely stretch', as Ian had called it, full of the uncanny. A hawk screeched, the sound echoing into the silence and making the hair on the back of my neck stand up. Several times I saw specters wafting about, their clothing ragged and bloody. I pulled my arms around my chilled body.

In the distance the ruins stood stark and somewhat forbidding, giving me the feeling that I was no longer welcome here. My mind conjured the former scenes of battles—screaming and the cries of pain, the metallic clash of swords, women and children scattering in the wake of the attack. All at once I wanted the bustle of town, my cozy hotel room, and the sound of laughter and conversation, electricity and a warm shower. Why Owen had taken himself off like this I didn't know.

I called out twice more just to make sure, waiting in the eerie silence for his answer, but when nothing happened I got into the car and drove slowly away. It began to rain, the large drops landing on the windshield and sliding down like tears. I searched as I went, hoping to see him walking along the track, or climbing down from one of the hills, but there was no sign of him. Once I reached the main road I headed back the way I knew to go.

By the time I reached the hotel I had worked myself into an even worse frenzy, sure that Owen had fallen into a ravine and was lying unconscious somewhere. Why hadn't I searched longer? I was about to drive back out when Ian arrived, meeting me just as I was heading toward his car. I saw Catriona driving away, her hand waving out the window.

"I guess you were wondering what happened to your car," I began, but he interrupted me.

"No worries on that account, lass. I thought perhaps ye would like to resume my services." He looked around. "Where did Owen take himself off to?"

"You tell me. We spent the night up there in the back of beyond, in some cottage he intimated belonged to him. And when I woke this morning he was gone." When Ian stared at me quizzically my cheeks burned. "He—we—"

Ian held up his hand. "Nae need to explain. I could tell how ye two felt at dinner."

"I'd hoped I'd find him here with you. I was just about to go back and search some more."

"Shall we take ourselves to my house and sit down with a cup o' tea? I can see yer in no shape for sightseein'."

"But what about Owen?"

Ian was quiet for a moment, his gaze in the far distance. "Owen can take care of himself."

In the kitchen Catriona stood in front of the stove, an apron tied around her ample hips. She turned when I arrived, a smile lighting up her tired eyes. "Would ye care for some breakfast?"

I shook my head, not wanting to inconvenience her any more than I had to. I wasn't sure why Ian had brought me here. It seemed more important to go up to the ruins and comb the area for Owen. "How are you feeling?"

"The tests were all negative. I do not have ovarian cancer."

"I'm so glad to hear that."

"We all are," Ian said, moving to stand beside her. She looked up at him, love shining in her eyes. "Owen has gone missin'," he said quietly. They exchanged a significant look.

"What happened between ye two yesterday?" Catriona asked me, her brows pulled together.

My face grew hot again as I relived our night of passion. "Um—we—he, Owen seemed to think we were married in the past. We spent the night in a cottage some distance from the ruins. He snared a rabbit and cooked it over the fire. We ate."

"And did ye recall any of yer life together?"

"I had a dream a few nights ago, and when we were together yesterday I remembered a lot more. I've never had an experience like that."

Ian nodded. "The laddie mentioned something to us before he took ye up to the castle ruin. He was happier than I've seen him in a long time."

"He told me he recognized me the minute he saw me. I felt something right away too. And even weirder still, past life Owen, is the one who killed Finlay, my ghost back in Ames. Did I tell you I came here on Finlay's behalf? And now the case is solved and he can move on."

"So, ye ken, then."

I frowned. "What?"

Ian slanted a glance toward Catriona who spoke. "Ye ken that Owen is not a normal man, Summer." She turned to pour me a cup of tea and handed it over.

I laughed, taking the cup into my hands. The pungent steam wafted upward. Earl Grey. "Normal is not a word I would ever use to describe him, no. But where is he? I hope he didn't end up with a broken leg or something. I should try to find him, don't you think? I wasn't going to leave, but I got spooked. There's an eerie energy up there."

Catriona brought over a plate of what looked like scones and set them down. "So when ye said the case is solved and he can move on, ye weren't referring to Owen?"

"No. I was talking about Finlay Ross McCloud, the ghost who asked me to find out who killed him. As I said, it was Owen in his previous life who murdered him. In that life Owen and I were married and had two children. Finlay was my great-uncle. Owen was a Mackenzie and I was a McCloud and Finlay couldn't handle me being with him—at least that's how Owen tells it." I took a sip, waiting for their reply, but neither one spoke. "Finlay has been camped out in his son's grave in Ames. Do you have any idea how a ghost could die here in Scotland and end up in the States?"

Ian gave me a look I couldn't interpret. "Ghosts dinna move around like normal folk, Summer."

"I think Finlay thought the grave was his, but when I checked out the dates it would have been impossible—his son of the same name lived to be ninety five."

"So he's confused."

"Apparently so. From our conversations he has no idea it isn't his grave. I think he got mixed up between his life and his son's life."

"More than a hundred years of waftin' about in spirit form can do that to a lad," Ian chuckled. "Perhaps the name on the stone confused him."

I had a sudden feeling of urgency in my stomach, as though every moment counted. "Don't you think we should go back up there and look for Owen? I know you said he could take care of himself, but it seemed off to me how he disappeared like that...and the house..." I thought of the profound changes to the cottage when I woke up this morning. "The cottage was bare and cold this morning. Last night it was..."

"Like it would have been years ago?" Catriona interrupted.

"Well, yes. How is that possible? Did I slip into the past with him?" I shook my head, trying to laugh, but nothing came out. They both gazed at me without speaking. "What do you know that you aren't saying?"

"He cared very deeply for you, Summer," Catriona said gently.

"Cared...that's past tense."

"We thought you'd figure it out, lass, especially with your gifts and all."

I stared at the two of them, the truth finally dawning. "Owen is a ghost?" I whispered.

Ian nodded. "By your description of the cottage and what happened between the two o' ye, I would say he's moved on."

"But why now? How long has he been here?"

Catriona put her hand on my arm. "A very long time, but there was something he was waiting for. And I think he found it."

"He was waiting for me." I pondered that for a long

moment, feeling suddenly cold inside. "I should have known."

"He must have found peace," she added.

I thought of our intimacy, our tears, and the changes within the cottage. Somehow we *had* gone into the past. What happened between us was his way of saying goodbye. "*That's* why you called him the local loony."

"Aye, lass."

"But he looked so normal with his corduroys and sweater, the worn boots."

Ian chuckled. "He was wearing a filthy and ragged plaid the first time we set eyes on him, with a bloody sword strapped to his side. And his feet and legs were bare. When he never changed his clothes I made him dress in normal kit so the authorities wouldn't lock him up."

I had a sick feeling in my belly. "You don't think he'll come back."

Ian tilted his head, gazing at me with sympathy in his eyes.

"What about a grave? If there is one, I would like to see it."

Ian and Catriona exchanged a look and I saw Ian give a slight nod. "'Tis in a local churchyard. I can take ye there if ye like."

"Was this another life for him, or was he the same Owen, the one who…?"

"The one who loved ye and was yer husband? He was never able to have another life, Summer. Not until now."

"Are you sure? Did he say he would be moving on?"

Ian shook his head. "He only said if he didna see us again, not to miss him."

"When did he say that?"

"Yesterday mornin' before he took my car to escort ye up to the ruin."

I wiped my eyes, my thoughts on the night before. Maybe if I'd held back...maybe if we hadn't...he'd still be here.

Catriona put her hand on my arm. "He told us years ago that he'd died without saying goodbye to the one woman he loved. He had given up hope until you arrived."

"But why would he leave me like this?" I was blubbering now and Catriona handed me a tissue.

"'Tis the way of life, Summer--everything dies, everything is reborn. It was his time long ago, but he couldn't move on without layin' eyes on ye one more time."

I put my hand on my belly. I'd stopped taking birth control a few weeks before the trip.

Catriona watched me with a perceptive gaze. "Owen could nae father a child in his state."

"Oh," I said, my face reddening and the tears coming faster. "How do you know?" I finally asked after blowing my nose.

"He was not of this world; even if he felt real there was a part of him that was never here."

When the silence dragged out Catriona picked up the plate and pushed it toward me. "Ye canna leave without tasting my bannock recipe. This is a plain one, but I've made them with dried fruit as well." She moved the butter dish my way.

When our eyes met I knew she was trying to distract me, the look on her face telling me it was time to come back to the present. I took a cautious bite. "Bannock is what they ate back then, right?"

"'Twas always a staple. It has a lot of nutrition. If ye come back for breakfast ye can taste my porridge."

"Come, lass," Ian said a few minutes later, taking hold of my arm. "Let's take a look at the churchyard. I'll try and answer any questions ye may have."

I put my teacup down, said goodbye to Catriona, and followed him out the door, the rest of the bannock in my hand. I took another large bite before I got in the car. Somehow Catriona's energy had come into the oatcake, my tears drying as I chewed.

CHAPTER THIRTEEN

The churchyard stood next to an old stone church still in use. It was some distance from town, in an area of oak and ash, some ancient beech trees spreading their limbs along the rickety fence that enclosed it. The older section was overgrown with weeds and ivy, many headstones either cracked and broken, or crumbled into small bits. The newer part was well tended, the small church behind, lovingly repaired. When we came to Owen's grave I saw that the grass around it had been cleared, the moss and lichen on the weathered stone chipped away to reveal the inscription.

Owen Mackenzie

1695—1722

"He was so young!" I gasped. "What does that mean?" I asked pointing to the nearly unreadable Gaelic words under the date.

Ian smiled. "I asked him the same thing. The translation seems to go along the lines of, 'I won't rest until I find my love', or something like that."

"Me...until he found me? He said Aine died before he did. Why would he want those words on his headstone?"

"He told me he was sure he'd see her again. He

believed in reincarnation."

I nodded slowly as understanding dawned. "I was Aine to him." I turned away to hide my tears.

"Dinna cry, lassie. The lad has finally moved on."

When Ian walked away I lowered to my knees in front of the stone, pulling out a few vines that would soon encroach. My tears fell as I said my own whispered goodbyes. "I wish you well on your travels," I finally murmured, taking in a heaving breath before rising. I went to join Ian who was having a smoke behind a large oak tree. "Has his ghost been here since he died?"

"He never said. Our first encounter with him was right here around five years ago. 'Twas after church, when Catriona and I were wanderin' about in the graveyard. We had nae idea what he was—'twas goin' on six months before he revealed himself."

"Did you believe him?"

Ian chuckled. "We did when he faded away right in front of our eyes--that and the filthy plaid he always wore."

"He told me he'd known you for centuries, but at the time I thought he was kidding."

"Not us personally, but maybe some past lives I'm nae aware of." Ian stared off into the distance.

"You'll miss him too."

"Aye, we will."

When we reached the car Ian turned to me. "What now, lass? Have ye solved all yer mysteries?"

"I know who killed Finlay, if that's what you mean.

144

But now I have to deal with my feelings for Owen and resigning myself to never seeing him again."

"'Tis a burden, to be sure. But if ye can think of it as a gift ye gave him, maybe ye can feel better about it all."

I nodded, but I knew it would take some time to process. "Could you drop me off at the hotel? I need some time alone."

Ian nodded and put the car in gear. "Ye are welcome at our house anytime, Summer. Just let Mairi know if ye wish me to drive ye anywhere, or ye'd like to join us for a meal. Catriona has taken quite a fancy to ye."

As soon as Ian dropped me off I walked down to the beach, my gaze sweeping across the expanse of dark water that stretched toward the horizon. Gulls screeched above me, the wash of gentle waves filling in the gaps between the raucous cries. Despite the cold I took off my shoes and socks, leaving them by a log that had washed in. I dug my toes into the wet sand as I walked slowly along, the aroma of salt and fish mingling in my nostrils. Several fishing boats caught my eye in the distance, bobbing in the waves, their nets strung out behind them. I looked back the way I'd come, my footprints meandering in a waving line—the only ones on a cold day like today.

I let my mind go free, not attempting to stop the emotions that whirled through, one after the other. Sadness was followed by a deep despair, followed by anger, followed by a resignation that felt so heavy I could barely lift my feet.

I was tired by the time I found my shoes again—

tired and chilled, my heart like a heavy stone in my chest. The tears had dried on my face, the salt of them mixing with the fine mist wafting in from the sea.

When I got back to the hotel I hurried up to my room, sure that my face was red and swollen from all the tears I'd shed. I stripped off my clothes and stepped into the shower, letting the hot water sluice down my back for a long time. Why hadn't he told me the truth and said a real goodbye? But I knew why. It would have been a hundred times more painful if he'd explained it all. As Catriona said, he was not of this world. It was amazing that we'd had any time together—how often does a living person have a love affair with a ghost? But despite the knowledge of why it happened, I was still devastated.

When my cell phone rang I jumped, the bright tone seeming wrong in the past place where I'd been. I grabbed it off the dresser and slid my finger across without checking to see who it was.

"Are you all right?"

"Jerry? Yes, I'm fine—why?"

"I had a dream that you were with some other guy. It was…"

I was surprised when I heard his voice catch. "What time is it there?"

There was a sound like sniffling and then he said, "I don't know—three or four a.m.? I couldn't go back to sleep after the dream."

"Tell me about the dream, Jerry—did it seem in the past or was it in the present?"

"Not sure, to tell you the truth. The guy you were with had long hair and was dressed in clothes that seemed archaic. I was a soldier and you were—not sure who you were, only that I saw you with this dude and I came unglued."

"How's your mom?"

He let out a long exasperated sigh. "She's just like she always is—a raving bitch who wants to run my life."

I smiled to myself. "Did you find out who did those things you accused me of?"

There was a moment of silence before Jerry said, "Yeah, she admitted it after I grilled her. You were right about all of it. Apparently she has some old contacts of Dad's to do her bidding."

"Did she apologize?"

"Hell no! Sorry is not in her lexicon. She said it was for my own good--

and she's been trying to fix me up. I'm sorry, Summer. Chances are you won't forgive me, but—"

"We should probably not discuss this on an overseas call, Jerry. I'll be back in a few days."

"Are you having a good time?"

I thought about that for a moment. "I don't know if I'd call it a good time, but it certainly has been interesting. I think I solved the case."

"Good for you. I want to hear about it as soon as you get back."

When I hung up I felt like I must have imagined the phone call. Jerry had called me long distance because of a dream? And the dream sounded strangely true, as though he was clairvoyant. Jerry had always made light of what he called my 'sensitivities', the word spoken in a sarcastic tone. And the statement he'd made about his mother was very surprising.

I stood in the middle of my hotel room realizing that I felt no guilt about what had happened between Owen and me. Normally making love to another man would have sent me into paroxysms of self-condemnation. But Owen was a ghost, and what had happened was related to the distant past.

I thought of Jerry and what we had together before his mother poisoned his mind against me. How could I be with a person who was so easily manipulated? And right now I was still caught up with Owen, despite knowing I'd never see him again. When I stared at my reflection in the mirror I saw a shadowy image behind me. Owen was still around. "Why did you leave me?" I whispered, willing his image to grow solid. But instead it melted away until there was nothing there.

The rain had begun again, the sound of water dripping from the eaves reminding me of weeping. I lay down on the bed, my mind going from Jerry's call to Owen and back again. And then I was up and pacing, my thoughts scattering like so many pieces of flotsam. My body felt like a prison cell as emotions came and went, leaving me drained and exhausted. I had a feeling of suffocation as I thought of him out there in the ether— completely gone from me. "Owen!" I shouted, a moment later whispering, "At least say goodbye."

CHAPTER FOURTEEN

"But why didn't the gravestone have the full date of his birth and death?"

The woman at the museum brought her attention back to my face. "Many times the exact dates were unknown. This man, Owen Mackenzie, or his relatives, must have held some sway in order to have anything further engraved on his stone. There is a strong possibility that he isn't even buried there. Back then family members often added gravestones to memorialize their loved ones who hadn't had a proper burial. "

Maybe he wasn't even there—did Ian know this? When I'd cried over the grave I hadn't felt Owen's presence. "You said all the records from the church are filed here now. Is there any way you could look him up and see if there's more information on him?"

"I don't have the time, dear, but if you wish to go through the files 'tis fine by me."

I moved behind the desk, following her into the back room where an enormous array of filing cabinets sat against every bit of wall space.

"What year did you say he died?" she asked.

"Born in 1695, died in 1722."

She pointed me toward a file. "Ye should be able to

locate him in there."

"Thanks." I watched her head out the door into the other room before I opened the file dated 1650--1750. The records were old and brittle, with nearly unreadable handwriting scribbled across the yellowed pages. It took fifteen minutes before I came upon the name Owen Mackenzie. But I couldn't decipher the rest of what was written. I pulled the sheet out of the file, leaving the spot open in order to replace it properly, and carried it into the other room. "Can you read this?" I asked, holding it out and pointing to his name.

She pulled on her half glasses and took it from me, holding the paper carefully between thumb and forefinger. "Hmm...yes, now I can make it out. 'Owen Mackenzie--killed while escaping prison...'. Here the writing fades, I'm afraid." She looked up. "I would surmise that it was one of the many clan skirmishes, my dear. This man was a Mackenzie and there were many other clans who fought against Clan Mackenzie at that time." She smiled and handed it back to me.

"Is there any record of his children--their names? His wife's name was Aine."

"Well, let me see." She took the paper again and scanned down. "Yes, here it is. Two children, Annie and Ross." She looked up. "His wife died earlier."

"Yes, I knew that."

A couple came through the door and she handed me the paper. "Make sure you place it exactly where it was."

I looked it over once more before I put it back in the file drawer. There was no mention of who wrote the words on his gravestone, or how they'd known what to write. I wondered if he'd put the words on the stone himself once he began hanging around Dornoch. The engraving had seemed newer than on the original dates and also less professional. For a moment I say him crouched in front of the stone with a tool in his hand, picking out the words.

On my way out of the museum I saw the woman from the plane again. This time she stopped when she saw me. "You're still here? Did you find what you were looking for?"

I wanted to ask her how she knew I was looking for anything, but I didn't. "Yes, I did. How about you? I noticed you had a book on ghosts, and I saw you up at Ardvreck castle a few days ago. According to legend there are a lot of them hanging around the ruins."

"I've been searching for my roots," she said. "You see, I'm a Mackenzie, and my family lived around here for years and years. In fact I'm certain there are many relatives of mine here now. As for ghosts—well—I do believe in them, but I have to say I haven't seen any on this trip."

"I'm a McCloud—Summer McCloud. Our families were rivals."

"Ah yes, Ardvreck Castle. But a distant relative of mine married a Macleod." She held out her hand. "I'm Annie," she said, "Annie Mackenzie."

I gripped her hand, feeling a shiver. "Was Owen one of your distant relatives?"

"Owen? I do recall reading about an Owen

Mackenzie who lived in the 1700's. He might have been the one who married a Macleod, now that I think about it. But of course Owen is not an uncommon name."

"Do you have any historical data on the two of them?"

"Why yes, I do. Would you like to see it?"

"I would, very much," I said, shivering all over. "All I could find in the museum were some unreadable church records."

"Are you at the Dornoch Inn?"

I nodded, not trusting my voice.

"I can lend you my book later on today if you promise to have it back to me by tomorrow. I'm leaving early the day after."

The same day I was leaving. "What time?"

She looked at her watch. "I should be back at the hotel by five this evening—is that too late?"

"That's perfect. See you then."

I spent the rest of the day wandering around Dornoch, my mind on Owen, Jerry, and the book Annie had. Was it odd that her name was the same as Aine and Owen's daughter? Names were often passed down through generations. In a little gift shop I bought an embroidered Clan Henderson coat of arms for Becky, and found a black cashmere scarf for Agnes. By the time five o'clock rolled around I was anxiously waiting in the lobby.

"There you are!" Annie said brightly, arriving through the front door. She reached into her bag and pulled out a leather bound book. "Here it is, but please be careful with it. It is old and very valuable, at least to me."

I took it from her, feeling a tingle as it came into my hands. "How did you come by this?"

"It's been passed down through my family, sort of like the family Bible. But it has been printed in the past hundred years." She laughed. "The first accounts were hand written on parchment—can you imagine that?"

"You're very lucky to have this. I'll take good care of it."

In my room later I read about Mackenzie history and Owen's place in it. Clan Macleod had arrested him after he beheaded Finlay Ross Macleod with a claymore sword. The account went on to say that Owen held Finlay personally responsible for his wife, Aine's, death. Owen managed to escape his imprisonment only to be killed a week later by another Macleod avenging Finlay's death. No name was given, but the killing had been brutal and Owen's death had been protracted. He'd been tortured. No wonder he hadn't been able to move on. I saw him in my mind's eye, crouched in front of the fire, shadows moving across his features from the flames, and his mouth...oh, his mouth. I heaved out a sigh of pain and put the book down. Would I ever get over this? We'd only been together a day and a night, but it felt like a lifetime.

I was deeply asleep, immersed in a dream that included Owen, when I suddenly couldn't breathe. When my eyes flew open Owen was bent over me, his fingers tight around my throat. His tears dripped onto my face as he squeezed. "I canna let ye go, lass," he sobbed. I gagged and clawed at him but he didn't release me. The corners of my vision darkened, colors swirling at the edges, and then there was nothing.

I woke again sometime later, my throat on fire. I rose and turned on the bathroom light, staring into the mirror over the sink, examining the redness and imprints of his fingers that still remained. It wasn't a dream—he'd actually tried to kill me. I sat on the bed contemplating the reason he would do such a thing. And yet he hadn't gone through with it—or had he left thinking I was dead? When I checked the clock it was three-thirty a.m.; there was no way I could go back to sleep after this.

I propped the pillows up behind me and stared into the darkness, hoping if I called to him he'd hear me. I was lightly dozing when I heard something stir, opening my eyes to see him standing at the foot of my bed. "Owen, why did you do that?" I asked, my voice cracking. My hands went to my throat.

He moved closer, his eyes dark as they stared into mine. "Ye called me to ye, lass. I was ready to move on, but the pull of ye is keepin' me here."

"That's why you tried to kill me?"

His eyes filled.

I reached for him, but my hand went right through his arm. "You're not solid!"

"Ye must let me go."

"But I love you—" Tears rolled down my cheeks.

"'Tis the same for me, but I am no longer of your world. Bein' with ye, sayin' goodbye, released me."

"I don't want you to go."

"Ye must get on with yer own life, lass. I canna be with ye." He stared at me for a long moment. "Tell Ian to take ye to yer grave," he whispered, his eyes locked with mine. I held on to his gaze as he became more and more translucent, until there was nothing left of him.

I turned my head into the pillow and cried.

Morning came too soon, my bleariness showing in the dark circles and puffiness around my red-rimmed eyes. Dreams had taken me across the moors, running crazily as I searched for Owen. But something inside had changed during the long night. There was no question now that it was over for good. I wouldn't see him again. And although I still felt heartbroken, I knew I had to return to my real life; as much as I cared for him, I would not have enjoyed being taken from it.

My phone rang as I was combing my hair, and when I looked at the screen it was Jerry again. "Jerry? What's happening now?"

"I spent another sleepless night because of you." His voice sounded grumpy and tired.

"In fact you're in the middle of it," I said, noticing the time.

"You've taken over my dreams, Summer. Have you

met some Highlander and fallen in love with him?"

"I have met a ghost," I answered truthfully. "But he's moved on now."

"A ghost—that's nothing new for you."

I wanted to say that having an affair with one was new, but I decided to keep that little fact to myself. "I guess not. I'm finding out a lot about the McClouds and the Mackenzies, and the clan wars. It was pretty brutal back then."

"And Finlay? You said you'd solved it."

"Jerry, why did you call me again? I told you I'd tell you all about it when I get back. Aren't you worried about your phone charges?"

"Actually I called to tell you I moved back into the cottage. I hope that's okay."

Was it okay? I had no idea. "We can talk about that the day after tomorrow."

"I wish I could come pick you up."

I laughed. "My car's at the airport."

"I know. What time do you get in?"

"Around three, I think, but I'll have to go through customs. I should be home by six."

"I'll make you dinner."

"How are my animals?"

"They were very glad to see me. I guess Becky left so early in the morning that Cutty got locked in a couple of times."

"What about the dog door?"

"Frozen shut."

"It's been that cold?"

"Cold enough to freeze a witch's—"

"Don't say it," I said.

"Can't wait to see you."

"See you soon," I answered, acutely aware that he was waiting for me to say the same thing. But my emotions were all over the place; I had no idea how I felt.

I called Annie's room to let her know I was in the lobby with her book. She was barely up and told me she'd meet me in the breakfast room in a half an hour.

"Good morning!" I heard her say, looking up from my cup of tea.

I held the book out. "I learned a lot from this. Thanks so much."

She sat down in the chair across from me. "You talk to ghosts, don't you?"

"How do you know that?"

"I saw you up at the ruin. You were talking and gesturing, but there was no one there."

"Yes. The woman had lost her child."

"I read about her in the papers I got at the museum. But I never saw her. Is there something special I need to do to see ghosts?"

I shook my head. "I think you either can or you can't. My entire town is filled with them, and everyone seems to see them. But most don't realize what they are."

"I envy you. I lost my husband recently and I hoped he'd visit me, but so far he hasn't."

Behind her I saw a hovering shape, a man with a receding hairline of spiky gray hair and kind eyes. "Does he have short gray hair?"

She stared at me, her eyes widening. "Do you see him? Is he here?"

"There is a man hovering around you. His hair is cut short and he's clean-shaven. He's wearing a tweed suit."

"That's him--that's my Harry!" She had tears in her eyes as she jumped up and turned in a circle.

"He's with you, and if you talk to him he may find a way to give you an answer."

"Thank you," she said, bending to hug me.

When she left I thought of our first encounter on the plane, her coldness. All of it could be attributed to losing her husband and the bitterness she felt. I vowed to stop making snap judgments about people.

After breakfast I stopped at the front desk to talk with Mairi. "Could you give Ian a call for me? I think we should leave for Glasgow sooner rather than later. My flight is very early."

Ian called the hotel by the Glasgow airport and made a reservation for me while Catriona made me a cup of tea and dished out a bowl of porridge. A pitcher of cream sat on the table and I poured a little onto the hot cereal, adding a teaspoon of sugar. It was good, but I barely tasted it as I sat at their kitchen table trying hard not to cry. I would miss them.

"Any more sign of Owen?" Catriona asked, sitting in the chair next to me.

I put my spoon down. "He tried to kill me last night." I pushed my turtleneck out of the way to reveal the marks.

Catriona's fingers traced my neck, her eyes wide. "What happened?"

"I must have passed out. He came back later to explain; he thought if he killed me…"

"You would always be together," she finished.

I nodded. "He said I had to let him go and get back to my own life." I took in a shuddering breath and went on. "I found out how he was killed and how he killed Finlay. He cut his head off with a sword."

"Oh my goodness," Catriona said, her hand going to her mouth. "I never would have thought our Owen—" Her gaze met mine. "But things were more violent back then, weren't they?"

I nodded. "The man who killed Owen tortured him. I read about it in a book one of the guests at the inn had with her. She's a Mackenzie."

"Aye. Annie. We know her from past trips. She lost her husband recently."

"She told me."

"And you say that Owen is gone for good now?"

"Sadly, I think he is. I don't know how I'll ever get over him."

"Once yer back home and in the swing of things ye'll be fine, lass," Ian said, sitting next to Catriona. "Do ye have a man in yer life?"

"I did. We argued before I left, and now…with Owen and everything—"

"Owen is gone and this other man is here with the livin'. Dinna lose yerself with a ghost, lassie."

"The woman at the museum seems to think Owen isn't buried in the churchyard. Did he tell you if his bones are there?"

Ian sighed, slanting a glance toward Catriona. "His bones are up in the hills where he died."

I frowned. "Owen wants you to take me to Aine's grave. Is hers close to his?"

"Aine and Owen are buried side by side, but I thought the marker in the kirk would be a more fittin' way to say goodbye. He chiseled the Gaelic himself."

Just as I'd thought. "Is there time to see the real graves?"

Ian didn't seem too keen, but he agreed nonetheless. "If yer wantin' to get to Glasgow at any reasonable hour we should head out now."

I handed my empty bowl to Catriona. "The porridge was almost as good as the bannock, but not quite."

She smiled and gave me a quick hug. "Have a good trip home, Summer. I enjoyed spendin' time with ye."

"Thanks for everything," I said, a lump forming in my already raw throat.

I could see the ruins in the distance when Ian turned the car onto a narrow lane heading west. The hills rolled on, rising up to loom in front of us, the narrow track skirting around them. The sky was a flat mass of gray. "How did Aine end up buried with him?"

"He stole her body and buried her at a place no one would think to look."

"Stole her from where?"

"From wherever Clan Macleod was holed up at the time. 'Tis all gone to earth now."

The hills around us closed in, the track disappearing, but Ian kept driving, tires sliding across the tufted grass and mud, as his frown of concentration grew deeper. When he suddenly pulled the car over we were at the base of two hills, a narrow rock-filled valley rising between them. Rivulets cascaded down, meandering over rocks before disappearing into the tufted grasses at the bottom.

"If it rains before we are out of here ye may not make yer flight tomorrow."

I looked at the sky through the windshield. "It won't rain."

Ian let out a snort and opened his door. He led the way toward the valley, his boots slipping in the thick mud that had accumulated from the recent rains. I had on the wrong shoes, but I didn't complain, my pulse loud in my ears as we climbed steadily upward. The place was familiar. "I think I've been here," I finally said, stopping to catch my breath.

"Accordin' to Owen, 'twas a favorite spot for the two o' ye."

"I can't believe he didn't bring me up here," I muttered.

"It caused him too much pain, lass. He only brought me once."

After twenty minutes of climbing we reached a wide rocky ledge. Ian pulled himself up, moving along the outcropping until it opened into a sheltered grassy area. Small wildflowers were caught next to rocks, their tiny pink flowers protected from the cold and wind. A hill led upward behind where we walked, and I imagined it full of yellow and pink flowers, purple heather growing here and there in clumps. It would be beautiful once spring came. Around a corner a little hollow came into view where I spotted two small cairns of stone set close to the hillside. "Aine is here," Ian said, pointing toward the one on the right. "And Owen lies next to her."

"I understand how Aine ended up buried here, but how about Owen?"

"Accordin' to him, 'twas a kindly family member who brought his body to lie next to Aine."

I bent to place my hand on the rounded stones of Owen's grave, almost sure I felt his heat rising into my palm. Yes, he was here. "The cairns have been added to recently," I said, looking up at Ian.

"Aye. The lad has kept the graves as they were. If he hadna done so, there would be no sign of 'em now."

A moment later I was kneeling, my jeans soaking up the wet from the grass as I cried. My tears fell on the stones as I whispered to him, oblivious of everything around me.

I'd been here when the sun was hot on my skin, when the heather was in bloom, a blanket beneath us to shield our naked bodies from the heath. Owen and I had lain together on this very spot. It was where Annie had been conceived.

When I heard Ian's warning cough I came back from wherever I'd gone, my mind releasing the images from the past that crowded my mind. For a moment I thought I saw Owen hovering close, but when I tried to focus on him, the image faded away. "Goodbye," I whispered. I waited for a moment, listening to the wind moving through the grasses, expecting some sign, but there was nothing more.

I looked up to see Ian watching me. "Have ye said yer goodbyes now?"

I nodded, standing. "Thank you for bringing me here."

We took our time climbing down, the silence of the place offering up image after image of the past. I saw myself laughing, hand in hand with Owen, our bare feet nimble as we climbed. And I saw Owen carrying my shrouded body up those hills, his tears falling on the muslin wrapped around me. I didn't want to see this, didn't want to visit our past, but it was as if the place itself forced the visions on me. Once we reached the bottom I ran for the car. "It's about to rain!" I yelled.

Sure enough, the rain began just as we came onto the graveled track. "Yer a lucky one," Ian said, turning.

But I didn't feel lucky at all. I felt infinitesimal in a timeless world where life and death went by in the blink of an eye.

CHAPTER FIFTEEN

The trip home on the plane from London went by almost too quickly. The meal came after we'd been in the air for an hour or so, and after that I slept for a while. And when I woke again I found myself going over the trip and trying to process it all. I never saw Annie. She must have been on a different flight. I hoped she and Harry had found a way to communicate.

By the time I pulled up in front of my cottage around six p.m., I was sure I wasn't ready to face Jerry. But there was no putting it off, I thought, noticing his motorcycle parked in its usual spot next to the house. The night was very cold and clear, stars blinking blue in the velvet sky. I gazed at my familiar street, the trees that had lost all their leaves, the familiar houses with their Christmas lights already up, and the tiny plot of garden in front of my cottage where narcissus would emerge in a couple of months. I took in a deep breath. *This is home*, I told myself, willing the images of my past life to go away. *This is where I belong.*

Before I got to the door with my bag, it was flung open and Jerry emerged. His feet were bare, and he was wearing low-slung faded jeans and a V-necked black sweater. His hair was mussed, as though he'd been nervously running his fingers through it.

"You were accurate on the timing," he said, gazing at me warily. He moved to give me a hug and then thought better of it, grabbing my bag instead. Before we reached the open door, Cutty raced out, his enthusiastic barks making me laugh. "So, you missed me, did you little guy?" I bent down to rub his ears and then picked him up.

"He isn't the only one," I heard Jerry say from inside the house.

Once inside I set Cutty down and closed the door. Jerry had a fire going and I could smell roast chicken. He was in the kitchen now, an apron tied around his waist as he stirred something in a pot and opened the oven door to check on the chicken. I took off my coat and hung it up in the closet and then kicked off my shoes.

"Should be ready in twenty minutes or so," he said, turning. "Glass of wine?"

He held one out and I padded into the kitchen to take it from his hand, his fingers grazing mine. "Thanks. My internal clock has no idea what time it is, but the food smells good."

"We can talk for a minute by the fire," he offered cautiously.

"Okay." I headed to the couch and lowered onto it, my gaze going around the familiar room. Despite my nervousness about Jerry's and my relationship, it felt good to be home. "Where are the kitties?"

Jerry pointed to the basket on top of the cabinet in the kitchen. "They've been spending a lot of time up there," he said. "I've been leaving the heat pretty low in the mornings—it must be the warmest spot in the house."

"Their winter hideout."

Jerry settled into the chair and took a sip from his glass. "So tell me about your trip."

"Before I get into that, how's Agnes?"

"Big as a house. They've moved the due date up."

"When?"

Jerry glanced at the calendar hanging on the kitchen wall. "This week, I think."

"I have to call her!" I said, putting my glass down on the coffee table.

"Now? Dinner is almost ready."

When I left for Scotland Jerry and I were barely speaking—now he was fixing dinner like a househusband and not wanting me to call my best friend? The domesticity of it was a bit much. "I won't talk long, okay?"

Jerry harrumphed and headed into the kitchen again while I pulled my phone out of my carry-on bag and turned it on.

"Are you home?" Agnes asked without saying hello.

"I am."

"You promised to call me again, Summer, and I never heard from you."

"I'm calling now. Jerry said your due date has changed."

I heard her sigh. "They said if I didn't go into labor this week they would induce me this coming Friday."

"Wow. I'm glad I'm home. That's three weeks earlier

than they said the last time."

"Tell me about it."

"Listen, Agnes," I whispered, glancing at the kitchen to make sure Jerry wasn't listening, "having sex is supposed to help bring on labor."

"Are you crazy? I'm huge! And honestly, I doubt very seriously if Sam would do it, even if I begged him."

I chuckled. "I bet he would if he thought he was helping things along. Just tell him what I said and see how he reacts."

"Okay, I will. He's a wreck."

"Maybe by this time tomorrow you'll be heading to the hospital."

I heard her draw in breath. "And you'll be meeting me there if I am."

"Don't worry, I will."

"Dinner's ready," Jerry called.

"Got to go—Jerry's here and he cooked me dinner."

"About that—"

"I'll talk to you tomorrow, okay?"

"Okay—have a good night."

"You too," I said, brightly.

I heard her laugh just before she hung up the phone.

Jerry had served up our plates and brought them to the table. He'd lit candles and found two of my best cloth napkins. "This is nice," I said, sliding into the seat he held out.

He didn't say anything as he sat across from me, but when our eyes met I could see the confusion and worry that lay behind his calm expression. "What's new with you?" I asked, forking a piece of chicken into my mouth.

"Not much, considering my preoccupation with you."

"Why is that, Jerry? When I left you were furious with me and I thought we were broken up for good."

"Sam talked to me the day after you left, and after that I had a long talk with Mom. When she admitted what she'd done I felt like a jerk. I can't believe I let her sway me like that."

I looked at my plate, my appetite disappearing. "I kind of decided that..." I looked up, meeting his gaze, "I can't be with a man who can be manipulated that easily."

His eyes darkened. "One little slip-up and you're calling it quits?"

I put my fork down. "Jerry, you've done this before. Your mother runs your life, whether you choose to recognize it or not."

His eyes narrowed. "Not any more she doesn't. I told her about us, and told her to stay the hell out of my business—that if she didn't she wouldn't see me at all."

"What did she say to that?"

"She cried and apologized, said that she'd only done what she did to save me from myself."

"Save you from yourself? In other words, she doesn't trust your judgment, especially when it comes to women."

"I guess so, but it doesn't matter anymore. I'm committed to you."

I pushed my chair back and carried my nearly full plate into the kitchen, crouching down to place it on the floor for Cutty. He hurried over, his tail wagging.

When I stood Jerry was right behind me, his hands going to my shoulders. "I love you, Summer," he whispered in my ear.

I wriggled away. "That's what you said before all this stuff happened with your mom, Jerry. I need time to process the changes. I don't think I'm ready to take up where we left off."

"You want me to go?"

I nodded, tears filling my eyes. I was overwrought, jet lagged, and still mourning Owen. There was simply too much going on for me to fall back into old habits. "Call me in a few days and we can talk."

"Something happened over there. You seem stand-offish and remote."

"When I left a week ago you were living with your mother. Now you want me to act like nothing's happened? Yes, many things happened over there, but that isn't why I need a few days to myself."

He nodded, his mouth in a thin line. I watched him stride into the bedroom, coming out with a bag a few minutes later. He glanced up at the counter where his espresso machine stood. "Shall I leave it or take it?"

I smiled despite myself. "Leave it for now. Are you going to your house, or to your mom's?"

"I'm not going back to Mom's. And my house is closer anyway." He gave me a crooked smile.

"Thanks for understanding, Jerry." He let me hug him, his arms coming tight around me.

"I wish we'd already had our talk and things were

good between us," he whispered.

I pulled away. "Patience," I said, moving to open the door. He grabbed his leather jacket and put it on, giving me one last lingering look before heading out. I listened to the familiar roar of his motorcycle coming to life, the sound fading as he took off down the street. I was crying now, despite knowing that this was the right thing to do, both for myself and for him. I put the food away and cleaned the kitchen, the familiar actions soothing something deep inside. All I needed was a good night's sleep, I told myself when I'd finished. Unfortunately I didn't believe that little voice of reason.

'Where are ye, lass?' The words wafted toward me from the open window where a light breeze had come up. 'I'm here, Owen,' I called out. But when I went to the window it was snowing outside and the warm breeze had turned into a heavy wind filled with ice crystals. Owen was there, a wide piece of wool fabric wound around his body and over one shoulder. His bare feet were blue with cold and the snow had turned his hair white.

I woke shivering, freezing wind blowing in from the window behind my head. I moved to shut it and grabbed another blanket out of my antique cupboard. My mind hovered in between dreaming and waking. I wondered if I'd really heard Owen, or whether this was merely a dream. The scent of Jerry's after-shave was all over the pillow, the familiar spice sending me into another bout of tears. I still loved him, but before I could be with Jerry again I had to come to grips with my feelings for Owen. How could I be caught between a real live, flesh and blood man, and a ghost?

CHAPTER SIXTEEN

I woke with an intake of breath, unsure where I was for a second. I was wrapped up like a mummy in the bedclothes, only my nose sticking out, with Cutty glued to my side. The heat must have gone out during the night. I jumped out of bed, pulling the blanket with me as I headed to the thermostat. But when I reached it I realized that the electricity was off. Snow had fallen and was still falling, the scene outside like a winter wonderland. Every tree branch was encased in ice. I went to the fireplace, very glad that Jerry had carried in a load of wood the night before. Kindling was chopped neatly and there were several newspapers to be used as fire starters.

Once the fire was going I heard plaintive meows, looking up to see the cats emerging from the basket. They jumped down and greeted me with purrs and then begged for food, both of them rubbing against my legs. I rubbed their ears. "Okay, I'll feed you."

Once the cats and Cutty were fed I checked my phone, surprised to see that it was nearly ten a.m. Good thing I hadn't planned to go to Tarot and Tea today. I hadn't even thought to ask Agnes about my store the night before. It was then that my phone rang.

"Summer, Agnes is in labor!" Sam shouted

frantically. "I'm coming to pick you up."

"I'm not dressed yet, and..."

"Well, get dressed. She said if you weren't there she'd kill me."

I laughed. "I'll be ready when you get here."

I was dressed and had slugged down a cup of espresso before he arrived, his heavy knock rattling the windows. When I opened the door his eyes were wide with nerves.

"This is a first baby, Sam. It'll take hours. Nothing to worry about."

"I took her in at two a.m., Summer, after her water broke. The nurse seemed to think she was well on her way. She was six centimeters dilated when I called you."

"How did it happen so quickly? When I talked to her last night she said--"

Sam grinned and grabbed my arm and dragged me through the snow to his idling cruiser. "We took your advice."

Agnes was having a contraction when I walked into the room, her face flushed and sweaty. "If someone had told me how painful this was going to be I wouldn't have done it," she said between gritted teeth.

I glanced at Sam who had a crestfallen expression. "Yes, you would have, Agnes." When I moved to the bed to take hold of her hand she gripped me so hard I almost let out a yell. But a moment later her hand went limp. When I turned to Sam he'd left the room. I added a pillow behind her back. "It helps to breathe. We should have practiced this, but I thought we had time. Short rapid breaths when the contraction starts."

"I know that," she said sharply "I wish this was over with. Maybe I should have gone for the cesarean."

"No, Agnes. It isn't good for the baby, and it takes forever to heal from it." But she was in the throes of another contraction and hardly heard me. A moment later the nurse was peering between her legs. "Time to take her to the operating room," she said brightly.

"Operating room? Agnes wants to have this baby naturally."

The nurse looked up from where she was fiddling with the bed mechanisms. "There's no natural birth here at this hospital."

"What? Why not?"

"Liability," she said, unlocking the wheels of the bed.

"What do *you* want, Agnes?" I asked, grabbing her hand.

"I want the baby to come out of me, NOW!" she shrieked.

"But do you want the pain meds and all the other stuff they want to hook you up to?"

"No," she said, giving a grunt. "Just help me get him out!"

"This is unprecedented," the nurse said. "I'll have to consult with the doctor."

A few minutes later an annoyed doctor appeared in the room. "If you don't do what I tell you your baby could die," he told Agnes, his eyes narrowed.

"That is bullshit!" I yelled. "Who gives you the right to scare her like that? She's a perfectly healthy woman, and childbirth is the most natural thing in the world!"

"I'm not scared," Agnes said, her clear gaze going to the doctor. "My doctor told me I could have a natural birth."

"And who is that?"

Agnes gritted her teeth as another contraction began. "Her name is Naomi, Naomi Fielding," she managed to grunt before letting out a scream.

The doctor gave me a smug look. "Naomi Fielding has no connection with this hospital, which explains the confusion." He turned to the nurse. "Get the anesthesiologist in here ASAP. We need to get her prepped."

Agnes gave a shriek and kept on screaming, her breath coming in little gasps. "She's dilated nearly nine centimeters," the doctor said, examining her. "It's nearly too late to move her." He pushed the bed forward and called for the nurse who had suddenly disappeared. "Tell him to meet us in the OR!" he yelled out.

I had my hand on his arm to restrain him when Sam appeared, his face ashen. "What's happening?"

"This is the wrong hospital, Sam. Agnes wants a natural birth and this man—he wants to hook her up, give her pain meds, and I don't know what all!" I shouted.

"I did not say that!" the doctor shouted back.

"Then why did you just call for an anesthesiologist?" A second later Agnes screamed so loud that we all turned to face her. She was on all fours on the bed, sweat pouring from her narrow face. "The baby's coming," she grunted.

To my surprise Sam rushed to support her while the doctor went to see what was happening. "You need to lie down," he pronounced. "That way it's easier for me to do my job."

Agnes's face went bright red as another contraction moved through her. "It feels better this way," she managed to whisper.

The doctor grabbed her arm, pulling it out from under her and forcing her down. "Now get on your back," he hissed. He straightened and gazed toward the open door. "Where in hell is the anesthesiologist?"

Sam helped her back onto her hands and knees, his arms around her middle. "You can do it, babe," he whispered. "Breathe, just do your breathing." I could see Agnes relax with Sam there, her little breaths and grunts going on and on as she concentrated. "Okay, everyone needs to get out of here!" the doctor yelled, waving his gloved hands. "She's about to have this baby, and I don't want the field contaminated." He tugged at her hospital gown. "Lie down!"

"I'm not going anywhere," Sam said, staring him down. "And she doesn't want to lie down. Can't you see that?"

"What is going on here?" a female voice asked from the doorway. "I'm Doctor Fielding and this woman is my patient!"

"Naomi, you know the rules here. I can't let her…"

"What has changed you from a decent doctor into a bully?" she asked, moving him aside. "I take full responsibility for this woman, Jack. Now please move out of the way."

The doctor gave her a hostile look and strode toward the door. "If anything bad happens here I wash my hands of it."

Naomi flashed him a narrow eyed look. "It is all under control," she told him. She checked Agnes over, her gloved hands probing inside her gently. "Your baby is ready to be born, Agnes," she said quietly. "All we need to do now is monitor how fast he arrives. Can you do that for me?"

Agnes had no response to that and in the next second I could tell she was bearing down.

"Agnes, please hold back a moment or two now. You need to stop pushing."

"Listen to her," Sam whispered.

Agnes had her eyes closed, a look of utter agony on her face. "I have to—I have to—"

Naomi let a minute tick by and checked her again. "Okay, you can push now."

I saw the head emerge, the shoulders coming next. Naomi caught him as Agnes collapsed. "It's a boy," she announced before she did all the necessary things to cut the cord, making sure Agnes expelled the afterbirth. She was efficient and kind as she settled Agnes into bed. "I have to weigh him and clean him up," Naomi told her. "We'll be right back."

A moment later the white sheets of the bed turned dark from blood, Agnes's face going pale. I opened the door and yelled for the nurse who rushed in. In the next moment they wheeled her quickly away, leaving Sam and me standing there.

"What's happening?" Sam asked worriedly.

"They'll probably do a D&C," I answered.

"What's that?"

"Dilation and Curettage, a procedure to clean out the tissue that got left behind. I'm sure she'll be fine." I tried to keep the worry from my features.

Sam and I sat in the waiting room for over an hour, impatient for word of Agnes. When we saw Naomi coming down the hall we both stood. "She's fine," she said. "Your baby was big and your wife is small. These things happen. It's nothing to be worried about."

"Can I see her?" Sam asked, his voice cracking with emotion.

The doctor nodded, leading us back down the hallway to the room where Agnes rested.

Sam rushed to her, burying his face in her neck. They were both crying. I waited until he moved back a step before taking hold of her hand. "That was amazing," I told her.

"Both of you were amazing," she answered, a wan smile coming over her exhausted features. "Even with the bleeding I'm glad it was natural. At least I know the baby is free from chemicals."

"Where is the baby?" Sam asked, frowning.

A moment later the door opened and the nurse came in carrying a swaddled bundle. She placed the baby in Agnes's arms. Sam moved aside the blanket, he and Agnes both gazing down before their tear-filled eyes met. I had to leave the room. This was an intimate and private moment for the two of them.

I was in the waiting room when Jerry arrived. "How is she?"

"Sam's with her." I patted the seat next to me. "Wait here with me—they're having a moment with their newborn."

Jerry met my gaze, and the raw look of longing I saw there brought tears to my eyes. I didn't go with him when Sam came to get him, instead sitting alone with my arms wrapped tight around my body.

CHAPTER SEVENTEEN

"My dear girl! What a discovery! Have you spoken to the ghost about it yet?" Mrs. Browning peered at me, her bright eyes reminding me of an inquisitive bird.

"I haven't had time to go to the graveyard, what with the birth and everything." The store was unusually quiet at the moment, and when she'd questioned me about my trip I'd told her how Finlay was killed. I left out what happened with Owen. "How did Agnes do in my absence?" I asked, gazing at the orderly shelves, the new shipment of essential oils lined up neatly.

"She is a darling girl, so sweet and helpful. I told her she would make a wonderful gypsy fortune-teller with her coloring and dark hair. But now with the baby I'm sure she'll have her hands full."

"What about Valerie, Becky's mom? Is she still thinking about doing the Tarot?"

"She did come in one day and a few customers took her up on it. Unfortunately Becky is having some trouble down at the bakery and Valerie has been assisting her."

I stared at her. "What kind of trouble? She was house-sitting for me until Jerry—"

"Oh, that nice policeman—yes, she said he'd moved back in. Have you patched things up?"

I was saved from answering that question when Douglas arrived, his lined cheeks flushed from the cold wind. But I also hadn't had a chance to find out what trouble Becky was going through; we hadn't spoken since my trip. I would run down there at lunchtime.

For a ghost, Douglas gave me a strong hug, and then pulled back to scrutinize my face. "You seem changed, somehow. What happened up there in the wilds of Scotland?"

I glanced around at the other two customers who had just arrived, and Mrs. Browning eavesdropping from her place next to the goddess books. "I'll tell you all about it, but not right now." I gazed at him. "Have you met your grandson?"

Douglas grinned, an expression I'd never seen on his weathered face. "Yes, indeed I have. She's bringing him home today."

The baby had been born on Sunday—this was Tuesday morning. "So soon?"

"She's in good health and Sam is on maternity leave. She'll have plenty of help."

"I'm sure she'll be glad to be there. I'll have to stop by after work."

"Samuel is already quite perceptive. I wondered if he would be able to see me," he said, lowering his voice, "but he focused directly on my face, and if I'm not mistaken he gurgled with happiness."

"Gurgled with happiness? He's not even three days old!"

Douglas sniffed. "I'm only telling you what I observed. Newborns are closer to the ethereal, you know."

"Children and dogs," I muttered, thinking about Cutty and my graveyard ghost.

"Now, my dear, when will you tell me of your adventures? I've already heard that Jerry has been sent packing—was that because of your trip?"

"Who told you that?"

"When I asked after you at the hospital Sam mentioned it."

I had yet to tell anyone about Owen, and I wasn't sure who I wanted to share it with, aside from Becky and Agnes. "I wasn't ready to let him back into my life, not after what happened with his mother."

Douglas nodded sagely. "It is wise to wait until that situation is sorted."

"Sorted? That sounds like a Britishism."

Douglas shrugged. "Could be my British heritage creeping in."

"Ah yes, Weatherby."

"They came from close to West Yorkshire—'wether' is Norse for sheep and 'byr', now changed to 'by', refers to a farmstead. I was once a sheep farmer."

"You personally?" I asked, bending close.

"No, my dear." He chuckled. "I'm not *that* old."

When a customer headed toward the counter with a small brass figure of Ganesha to buy, I turned to help her.

During a lull I closed the shop, putting the shut sign up before rushing down the street to the bakery.

When I hurried in Valerie looked up from her place behind the counter. "Summer! Who is minding the store?"

"I locked it up. I heard that something was going on with Becky. What's happening?"

"Becky is—" Valerie stared into the distance. "Becky's old boyfriend appeared out of nowhere and she's taken off with him."

"What? She never mentioned a boyfriend."

"He's her first love, Summer. He used to be this sweet-faced boy who hung around the house. Now he's got a shaved head and tattoos all over his body—and he drives a Harley."

"You don't like him."

"I don't trust him! He has no money, no prospects. He's mooching off my girl."

"Becky has always been the salt of the earth. I can't see her being taken advantage of. Maybe she's…"

Valerie held her hand up. "She closed and locked the bakery and walked away. Does that sound like her? If she hadn't sent me a text, I would have had no idea. Now I'm trying to keep her business afloat until she comes to her senses."

I couldn't wrap my mind around this turn of events. "And you met him?"

"Of course I met him. Becky brought him by the house to reintroduce us. He was pleasant enough, but after they left, and I did the Tarot, I began to suspect that something else was on his mind."

"Like money."

"Like money and like the bakery. My daughter has done very well for herself, and the idea of him coming in and taking it over gives me a chill."

"Is that what the cards told you?"

"The cards told me that my Becky is lost. I got the lovers reversed and the hierophant reversed, both indicating that things are not right."

"Where have they gone?"

Valerie shook her head. "I have no idea. Becky said she'd be back at the beginning of the year. She didn't even ask me to watch the store! Did she think her customers wouldn't turn to some other place for their baked goods?" Her lips pursed. "Irresponsible in the extreme."

"I'd best get back. But if you hear anything, please let me know." I put my hand on hers. "I'm so sorry."

She gave me a wan smile. "I want to hear about your trip one of these days."

I nodded and hurried out the door.

When I got back there were several customers milling about my stoop who were glad when I opened the door. It was a frigid day, ominous clouds looming. I hoped the snow would hold off long enough for me to visit Agnes after work.

The afternoon went by quickly, my sales steady. But when it grew dark, and the store emptied out, I decided to close. I left the shop early, citing the weather on a small note taped to the window. I doubted I would have many customers at four-thirty in the afternoon.

Surprisingly, my car did fine in the snow still left on the road up to Agnes and Sam's house. When I parked I saw a few white flakes flutter out of the sky. I had to be off this hill before it began to snow in earnest, I thought, hurrying toward her door.

"Summer!" Sam held the door open, a smile of welcome on his even features. "Agnes is in the living room feeding little Sammie."

I went ahead of him, my gaze falling on Agnes in her warm black robe, the baby suckling at her breast. She looked like a Madonna with her dark hair fanned around the pale oval of her face, her expression serene. I sat next to her. "Looks like you got the hang of things."

She smiled. "Sammie never once had trouble latching on. He's a wizard already."

I glanced at Sam, wondering if this term might bother him, but his wide-eyed gaze was on his wife and his newborn. He looked spellbound and overcome with love. A moment later he seemed to come to his senses. "Would you like anything, Summer? I have an open bottle of wine, or you could have a beer."

"Wine, if you're having some. Are you drinking, Agnes?"

She moved the baby to the other breast. "Only beer for now. It's supposed to help with my milk supply."

Sam chuckled, eyeing her ample breasts. "Not that you need any help."

He disappeared into the kitchen, arriving a moment later with a beer for his wife and a glass of red wine for me. "Hope you don't mind, but Jerry said he'd stop by this afternoon. If I'd known you were coming, I'd—"

I felt a little twinge in my belly. "It's okay. It's not like we're enemies. I just need to regroup, that's all."

Sam had a worried expression that he tried to hide before heading off in the direction of the kitchen again.

"How is motherhood?"

Agnes chuckled. "It's better than the labor, although I'm not sleeping all that much. Sammie is on demand feeding for right now."

"Two a.m. and six?"

"More like eleven, one, three and five."

"That sounds like zero sleep, Agnes. Will you try and put him on a schedule?"

She shrugged, gazing down on his fuzzy head. "Sam's being so sweet, getting up and bringing him to me in bed for at least two of the nighttime feedings. He'll settle out, I'm sure of it."

I heard the click of the door and then Jerry's voice. "Sam? I'm here--can I come in?"

He closed the door behind him, but when he saw me I noticed the hesitation that came over his features. He took off his leather jacket as he moved into the living room, slinging it across the back of a chair. "Sorry, Summer. I didn't know you'd be here."

"Why is everyone so worried about it? We don't need to be kept apart, Jerry. I only wanted a few days to myself."

He smiled, his gaze going to Agnes who was in process of pulling the robe closed. "How is he?"

She held him out. "Take a look for yourself."

Jerry moved close and took the baby in his arms, a tender expression coming over his features as he gazed down. "So quiet and sweet. I thought they cried a lot."

Agnes let out a chortle. "Try coming around in the middle of the night."

"Beer, Jerry?" Sam called.

"Love one."

I sipped my wine, watching Jerry coo to the baby, his eyes going soft. When Sam arrived from the kitchen and held out the beer, Jerry stood and deposited little Sammie into my lap. I placed my wine glass down and moved aside the blanket to take a look. He had a fuzz of light hair like Sam's, his lashes dark against his very fair skin. He looked like an angel. "He's beautiful," I murmured. When I looked up Jerry was staring at me with the same expression he'd had on his face at the hospital. I had a strange feeling deep inside my belly, as though my womb yearned for a baby of my own. I quickly looked away, trying to hide the flush that rose into my cheeks.

A minute or so later Sam took the sleeping baby out of my arms and headed toward the bedrooms. "Time for bed, little guy," I heard him whisper.

"Not for long," Agnes said, taking a gulp of her beer. "He looks like an angel now, but believe me, the screeching that comes out of that rosebud mouth during the night is decidedly not angelic."

Jerry and I laughed, our eyes meeting again. This time he looked away first.

When I left an hour later Jerry walked me out to the car. "Can we get together—you know—for dinner, or coffee, or something? I need to talk."

The softly falling snow muffled sound, as though we were cocooned in a world of white. The silence was like a balm to my overwrought nerves. I turned to face him, my hand on the car door handle. "Maybe you could come by Sunday. Shall I call you mid-week?"

Jerry frowned. "I'd hoped, I mean, I thought..."

"What?"

He grimaced. "I was hoping for sooner than that. I'm going crazy, Summer. I miss you and I have to tell you some stuff."

"Why now all of a sudden? You didn't miss me when you were staying at your mom's."

His eyes turned dark. "How do *you* know?"

"I assumed you didn't since you were all ready to suspect me of terrible things."

"Can we not go over that again? I've apologized like a zillion times."

I smiled. "Not quite a zillion yet. I'm really busy this week catching up on the store and everything. Would Friday be better? We can have a glass of wine together."

He nodded and turned toward his motorcycle. I watched him swing his leg over and turn the key, my gaze still with him as he roared down the snow-covered street.

When he turned the corner at a precarious angle I had to shut my eyes. But there was no crash, or even the squeal of wheels.

I slipped into the driver's seat and sat there for a moment wondering if I would be ready to see him by Friday. There was something working in the back of my mind, and I wanted to see what it was before I got caught up in whatever was going on with Jerry. I should have stuck to Sunday instead of giving in to his sad puppy look. The apple didn't fall far from the tree.

I sighed and turned the key, the engine sputtering into its bumpy beginnings. I HAD to take the car in and find out what was going on. But when did I have time for that?

I was in bed by nine, the Celtic fantasy book I was reading falling into my lap and waking me when I dozed off. When did I ever go to sleep this early? I placed the book on the bedside table and turned out the light.

Jerry was dressed in a kilt, his hair long and tangled. A broadsword hung on his hip. He had a fierce expression on his face as he leaned in. "Give us a kiss, lass, for luck."

My eyes flew open. I rose from the bed and padded into the kitchen, Cutty on my heels. "What is going on?" I asked him as I heated up milk and stirred cocoa into it. "Is Jerry one of my past lives too?"

CHAPTER EIGHTEEN

The electricity was out in the morning, ice encasing the limbs that had been so soft with snow the night before. I picked up my phone to check for a weather update and then checked about power outages. The grid was down nearly everywhere and temperatures had plummeted. So much for living in a small town with outdated infrastructure.

"I guess that means no work today," I told Cutty, who stared up at me expectantly. I gazed out the window, watching the falling snow before finding a can of dog food to mix in with his dry. After coaxing the cats down from their warm perch and feeding them, I made a fire, huddling in front of it in my heaviest robe. It wasn't long before the house warmed up. I gazed sadly at the espresso machine. I had no way of making coffee.

It was around nine when I decided to take Cutty for a walk. I hadn't been to the graveyard since I arrived home; telling Finlay what I found out was long overdue. After banking the fire and putting up the screen, I pulled on my heaviest coat, a wool hat and gloves, and snow boots. When I clipped on the leash, Cutty was already doing his happy dance, twirling around me on his tiptoes.

As soon as we reached the graveyard I let Cutty go, opening the squeaking gate to let myself inside. The gravestones looked like puffy pillows, their edges obscured by the cover of white. I could hear the faint sound of twigs snapping as the ice took its toll. When I reached Finlay's grave I stood there for a while, wondering what I would tell him. How would he feel knowing that the man I'd loved in the past had killed him? Would he remember? Being in his son's grave all these years didn't indicate a recollection of past events.

"Finlay?" I whispered, wondering if he was only available after dark. But a moment later he appeared, as translucent as I'd ever seen him. But maybe that was due to the daylight.

"Hello, lass. What canna do fer ye?"

I frowned, wondering if he even remembered what we'd talked about. "I went to Scotland, Finlay, to find out who killed you?"

He looked blank for a moment and then brightened. "Aye. And what did ye find?"

"Well, for one thing, you're in the wrong grave."

"What are ye on about?" He shook his head, trying to brush the snow off the headstone, but his see-through fingers did nothing.

I brushed the snow off and then read what was written there. "Finlay Ross McCloud, 1789 to 1884. This Finlay was ninety-five years old." I looked up at him. "This is your son's grave."

Finlay looked confused, his head shaking in disbelief. "I've been here since I died, lass. 'Tis nae possible."

"Do you remember living here in Ames? Tell me one thing about this place."

"'Twas too long ago. How would I remember?"

"And yet you told me you were murdered. How did you know that?"

If a ghost could go pale, Finlay did. He stared into space at nothing for several long moments, his hand on his forehead. "One of those men I mentioned to ye killed me—which one was it?"

Now he was belligerent and a little bit scary. "You aren't going to like what I found out," I said, trying to prepare him. "You weren't a very nice person, Finlay. Elsbeth left you, and you stole another woman and her children away from her husband because he was a Mackenzie."

He raised his fist. "Clan Mackenzie! The bastards!"

I let a moment tick by, hoping the dark look on his face would lift. When he calmed and turned to me I continued. "It was that woman's husband who killed you, and for good reason."

He lunged for me, a look of hate on his features, but he fell right through my body. A moment later he was staring at me with narrowed eyes. "Yer lyin'. I was an honorable man. Elsbeth loved me."

"An honorable man doesn't destroy a marriage and let a woman die."

"What woman? Who did I let die? How do ye know all this?"

"Because I was the woman, Finlay. I am, and was a McCloud. In a former life I married Owen Mackenzie and we loved each other. You stole our children and me away from him and I died before we could reconnect. Owen cut off your head with a claymore."

Finlay was livid, his dark eyes flashing. "If I did such a thing 'twas because I loved ye. Was I yer father in this life yer referrin' to?"

"Great-uncle."

"Then ye were my responsibility!" he shouted. "I did what I had to do. That man had no right to ye, lass--no Mackenzie had the right to take ye from me!"

He was out of control now, and even though I knew he couldn't do me harm, I was scared. Cutty heard the shouting and began to bark, his sharp yips adding to the chaos. "I have to go," I said, moving backward away from the gravestone. "I did what you asked."

I stumbled, my hands scraping along the rough rock as I tried to stop my fall. When I righted myself I focused on the translucent form I'd left behind. Finlay thrashed around the grave making no prints in the snow, his dark look of hatred focused on me. I hurried toward the gate, turning back once I was through. He was no longer in sight. I was still shaking by the time I reached home.

I called Agnes, hoping she wasn't in the middle of a nap.

"Summer? What's wrong?"

"Why do you think something's wrong?" I asked, annoyed that my moods were so obvious.

"Because I saw you just last night when Jerry was here, and the two of you were acting weird, and...you never call me at this time of day."

"I didn't go to work today—the electricity is off everywhere."

Agnes laughed. "And that's the reason I'm hearing from you? Give me some credit here."

I heard the baby crying in the background and Sam's voice. "Do you need to go?"

"Sam's dealing with it. Now tell me what's going on. We haven't had a chance to talk since you got back."

"I just got back from Finlay's grave, and he's angry with me."

"A ghost is angry with you? How did he express this anger?"

"He was shouting, for one thing...I haven't told you what happened in Scotland."

"No, you haven't."

"I met the guy who killed him, Agnes...and I had an affair with him." I waited without breathing for her reaction to this bombshell.

There were several long moments of silence before she said, "You had an affair...with a ghost."

"It's a long story. He and I were married in a past life, and he's been waiting around for me so that he could say goodbye."

"And this goodbye—was it sexual in nature?"

"Well, yes, partly. But we loved each other—"

"In a past life."

"Yes, but I was pretty enamored with him in this life, to tell you the truth. He was a pretty cool guy."

"For a ghost."

"Yeah, I guess."

"This explains your behavior around Jerry and why you decided you needed time alone. Are you planning to tell him?"

"I don't know. Would he believe me? And also, you know how he is—he'd go ballistic if he knew."

"But the guy's gone now, right? Tell me the truth, Summer—did you really have sex with a ghost? I can't believe it's even possible."

"It's possible, believe me. We were married back in the seventeen hundreds. We had two children together."

"And that makes it all right?"

"Stop it, Agnes! I didn't call to get your permission—it's already done. I loved Owen way back when, and I guess those feelings rose up in the present. I can't help it!"

"Are you calling for my blessing, or what?"

"No! I called to talk to my best friend and tell her what happened to me in Scotland. And don't you dare share this with Sam!"

"I won't say anything...he wouldn't believe me anyway. Sorry for snapping, but when you were gone, Jerry spent a lot of time with us. He's in love with you Summer. He wants to..." I heard Sam yell in the background, Agnes's intake of breath. "Got to go, call you later."

I put my phone down and stared out the window. It was still snowing, and if I wasn't mistaken it was coming down heavier than before. When my phone rang again I was sure it was Agnes to finish our conversation, but instead it was an unknown number. Something told me to answer.

"Summer? Is that you?" a tinny, faraway voice asked.

"Becky? Where are you?"

"I'm…somewhere close to Boston. I need you, Summer. Can you meet me at the harbor?"

"Boston Harbor? Where? It's a big place."

"The Greenway Carousel."

"When? You do know it's snowing, right?"

"It isn't snowing here. Please come as soon as you can." The call ended, leaving me with a very uneasy feeling. For one thing, Becky never asked for help—she was a witch. And what I'd picked up in her voice was fear.

I put on my heavy coat and went outside, wishing I'd had my tires replaced. And what about my engine problems? What if I got stuck on the 95 somewhere between here and Boston? But then I heard Becky's frightened voice in my ear. She was definitely in danger. I went back inside, fed my dog and cats, and made sure the doggy door was unstuck. No hot coffee to take along, but I did grab a hunk of cheese out of the dark refrigerator, and a box of crackers and a bottle of water from the pantry. At least I wouldn't starve to death when the car slid on black ice and careened off the road into a snowdrift.

An hour and a half later I exited the 95 to get on route 93. Becky had been correct about the snow. It was like a dark cloud of misery hung directly over Ames. I let out a sigh of relief as I followed the directions from the mechanical voice coming from my cell phone. The woman wanted me to calm down—I could tell from her tone. For some odd reason my engine was humming along as though it had never had a problem. I began to wonder if it was linked into my psychological state.

When I drew close to the Greenway I followed the signs to public parking. I had to fork out ten dollars to park my car, but in the scheme of things it was hardly important.

It was disappointing that my first trip to Greenway Carousel was to pick up a distraught friend. I would have enjoyed wandering around, and maybe riding the thing, although with the weather I doubted it was open. It was famous, all the creatures that carried the riders were from local environs: Fox, squirrel, cod, lobster and grasshopper, joined falcon, whale, butterfly and turtle, as well as skunk, rabbit, oarfish, owl and harbor seal. I'd read all about the greenway project dreamed up by a woman philanthropist named Amalie Kass. It was done for the children of Boston and inexpensive to ride.

I walked quickly toward the colorful edifice in the distance, wondering briefly if I would find my friend, but there she was, her strawberry blonde hair standing out like a beacon in the muted gray light.

She hurried toward me. A second later she was crying in my arms.

"What is it, Becky? What happened? Your mom told me about the guy…your boyfriend? Is this about him?"

Becky pulled away and looked furtively over her shoulder. "If he followed me, I—"

I grabbed her shoulder. "What's going on?"

Becky's worried gaze met mine. "I didn't know what to do, Summer. You were the only person I could think of who would help."

"Your mom--"

"My mom doesn't drive when the weather's like this, and besides I don't want to give her a reason to say I told you so." She glanced at the ground as more tears spilled over. "Jacob's changed. He's into heavy drugs. He made me take them!"

"How could he make you? You're a witch!"

"My abilities were not up to his manipulations. And besides, I trusted him. He convinced me that it would be a spiritual experience. It wasn't," she added darkly.

"Where is he now?"

"I don't know. I left him passed out on the floor of the room we were sharing with his other druggie friends. I managed to slip out without alerting them, but if he finds me, he—"

"What? What did he do to you?"

Becky pulled her coat down to show me the bruises along her upper back. "He's a creep. I don't know why I believed him to begin with."

"You remembered who he was when you guys were first together."

She scoffed. "That was my first mistake. Mom thought he wanted to involve himself in the bakery. She saw right through him."

"Why did you come up here?"

"Because he wanted me to pay for his drugs, that's why. Of course I didn't know it at the time. I'm out several thousand dollars because of him, money I had saved for a rainy day." She met my worried gaze. "Can you take me home, Summer?"

"Of course! I think you should stay with your mom until we can report this creep and get him off the streets. If he comes looking for you again, he—"

"I won't fall for it again. And I'm already working on a couple of spells to keep him out of the bakery and out of my life." She gave me a wan smile.

"This reminds me of my brother—remember that fiasco?"

Becky shuddered. "I do. At least Jacob isn't torturing people."

"Only you," I said, peering closely at her tear-streaked face. My insane brother had lured women who looked like our mom to a cabin out in the woods, where he proceeded to torture and kill them. He was fixated on our mother, blaming her for all his psychological problems, and I had nearly been one of his victims. Another time when Jerry had come to the rescue.

I looked around, afraid I would see an angry and drugged-out man heading our way. I grabbed Becky's arm. "Let's get out of here."

On our trip home Becky showed me other bruises on her arms and chest where Jacob had beaten her. "He only did it when I refused to partake."

"Yuck," I said, glancing over at the purple and discolored skin. "Is he addicted?"

"He's a heroin addict."

"And you took it too?"

Becky nodded, her eyes filling again. "He forced me—hence the bruises. I was so sick afterwards I thought I would die."

I reached over to touch her arm. "I am so glad you called me."

She stared out the window. "I had a strong premonition yesterday that if I didn't get away from him I was going to die. He took my phone away and threw it in the river. I had to get a prepaid one to call you."

I glanced at her, glad I'd answered the call. Becky's premonitions were nothing to scoff at.

"To take you mind off things, you want to hear what happened to me in Scotland?"

Becky stared at me. "Yes, I do."

After I told her all about Owen and what had happened between us, Becky fell asleep, her head lolling against the seat. When I glanced at her I saw shadows beneath her eyes, her round cheeks sunken and hollow. She'd lost a lot of weight. I wanted to take her directly to the hospital to have her checked out, but she'd asked me to please take her home.

I parked the car in front of her dark apartment. "Are you sure you want to be alone?" It was after six, and leaving her there didn't feel right.

"Just for tonight, Summer. Tomorrow I'll call Mom and make a plan, but right now I want to take a long hot bath, climb into my own bed, and have a good night's sleep for once."

"What about food?"

"I have some frozen stuff—don't worry about me. I'm a witch, remember?"

I gave her a skeptical look. "Witch or not, you need help right now. I'm calling you first thing in the morning."

She smiled and opened the car door. I waved to her just before she disappeared up the stairs to her apartment.

CHAPTER NINETEEN

Everything was back to normal the following morning—at least in the way of electricity and clear streets. I had a vague feeling of unease that I tried to ignore as I made espresso and prepared to go to work. It was still too early to call Becks.

I made it to the store earlier than usual, using the extra time to call Becky on her cell. When she didn't answer I figured she was either in the shower or still asleep. But my insides churned. I called Valerie.

"Becky is home," I told her after we greeted each other. "I picked her up in Boston yesterday. Can you check on her? I tried to call this morning and she didn't answer."

"I'm down at the bakery, Summer. Is this important enough to close, do you think?"

I thought about that for a moment. "Yes, I think it might be."

"Okay. Thanks for letting me know."

At a little after nine my customers began to trickle in. "We missed you yesterday," Mrs. Browning said as she walked past my desk.

"It was snowing yesterday. Are you saying you were here?"

She smiled and waggled her graying eyebrows. "Some of us have other means, you know."

Ghosts were wafting around my store when I wasn't here? I began to answer her, but she'd already moved behind a tall bookcase. It gave me a peculiar feeling until I realized that it didn't matter much. They wouldn't steal from me, and what damage could they do? Unless they decided to use the front door and left it unlocked. I decided to warn her of this later. Right now I was too preoccupied with my friend.

My cell phone rang, Jerry's name on the dashboard. I hesitated for a moment before sliding my finger across the screen. "Valerie Henderson just called me," he said without preamble. "She seems to think her daughter's in trouble—told me to call you for the details."

"Becky got caught up with an old boyfriend who is definitely bad news. I called Valerie this morning because Becky didn't answer her cell."

"I'm standing outside her apartment right now. Thought I would check with you before breaking the door down."

"She doesn't answer? Is Valerie there?"

"She was here, but when she mentioned the bakery I told her to go—she didn't want to." I heard him sigh. "If something bad has happened I didn't want Valerie to be here."

"I'd say break it down, Jerry. I've had a weird feeling all morning. Will you call as soon as you do?"

"That depends on what I find."

I hung up, my stomach churning. If something happened to Becky...

"What is it, dear? You've gone all peaky." Mrs. Browning peered at me with her head to one side.

"It's Becky—something's wrong."

"Well, here's Valerie now," she said, gazing toward the door. But it was several minutes later before Valerie actually entered the store.

"Summer, have you heard anything?" she asked breathlessly after rushing to my desk.

"I talked to Jerry a few minutes ago. He's breaking in."

"Oh, dear gods," she said, her hand going to her mouth.

I moved from behind the desk to find her a chair. "He'll call when he knows something."

Valerie sat heavily, her gaze in the middle distance. "She's my only daughter. I should have done something earlier," she muttered. "This is my fault."

"What could you have done? She's a grown woman and needed to find out about Jacob on her own."

Valerie's tear-filled eyes met mine. "What did he do to her, Summer? What did that bastard do?"

Her shouts brought several looks from customers. I placed a hand on her shoulder. "He's an addict, Valerie."

"Did he hurt her?"

I looked down. "She has some bruises," I whispered, "but nothing serious."

I turned to help several customers who wanted to check out. After that I needed to pay some bills, take a quick inventory, and rearrange several shelves. When I glanced over my shoulder, Mrs. Browning was sitting in a chair next to Valerie, their heads together. By the time I finished checking the shelves, Valerie had gone.

It was an hour and a half before Jerry called me. "What happened?" I burst out before he could speak.

"I was about to tell you. She's in the hospital."

I sucked in breath. "Why—what happened?"

"She was passed out on the floor in the bathroom. I found needle marks, Summer."

"What? She can't be an addict--it doesn't happen that fast, does it?"

"There's a chance someone broke in and tried to give her an overdose, but I'm not discounting the possibility that she shot up last night. Hopefully the paramedics got to her in time."

"Hopefully." I was crying now, trying to keep my face turned away from the customers in my store. "Did you call Valerie?"

"Yes. If you want I can swing by after you close the shop and we can check on her."

"I'd appreciate that."

The rest of the day was a blur as I tried not to see my friend lying on her bathroom floor. I could barely concentrate when customers asked me questions, giving them the wrong change when they paid for things. At quarter of five I closed up, shooing one person out who had been browsing for over an hour.

I locked up and waited for Jerry, and when the cruiser arrived I ran for the passenger side. "Have you heard anything?"

He shook his head. "I've had a busy day with break-ins and all sorts of weird shit. It must be the holiday season coming; people tend to go a little crazy."

"I hope she's okay," I said in a small voice, turning to look out the window.

Jerry didn't say anything as he drove, too fast, toward the hospital. Luckily he was a cop so no one would stop him for speeding. When he parked I hopped out, waiting for him to lock it before the two of us hurried inside.

Jerry asked for Becky by name at the front desk and then steered me to the bank of elevators. "I'm sure they gave her naloxone," he said once the doors had closed.

"Naloxone—what's that?"

Jerry turned to me. "You do live in a bubble, don't you? It's a controversial drug that saves overdose victims, but also puts them into immediate withdrawal. It can be really bad."

"Do you think Becky would go into withdrawal after only taking heroin twice?"

Jerry gazed at me, all business. "It depends on how much she took, and how much she had in her system this time. She was out cold when I got there, with barely any pulse."

A chill raced through me. "Are you going after the guy who did it?"

"If I determine there is a guy, yes. I need to question Becky first."

"There's definitely a guy," I said, trying to get him to look at me. "She wouldn't shoot up—I'm sure of it." But he was in full cop mode, his gaze on the elevator doors.

Once the door slid open, Jerry strode to the front desk. I waited while he talked to the nurse there. After a moment he nodded to me and headed off down a long hallway. I ran to catch up. "How is she?"

His lips pressed together. "She's alive."

When we reached the room, Valerie was there, her face wet with tears. "The doctors gave her a drug to stop the effects, but they nearly lost her," she whispered. "Apparently Jacob really meant to kill her."

"Let's wait until we talk to Becky before making accusations, Mrs. Henderson," Jerry said. "Has she regained consciousness?"

"Barely."

I moved to the bed to look down on my friend. They had her hooked up to a machine to measure her pulse, heart rate and blood pressure, as well as a drip. "Becky?" I whispered.

Her eyes fluttered and opened. "Summer," she croaked, her hand going to her throat. "What happened?"

"We were hoping you could tell us," I said, glancing at Jerry who had moved to my side.

"Did you shoot up, Becky?"

I frowned and grabbed his arm. "Jerry, she--"

"No," she mumbled. "It was Jacob, I'm sure of it. I was getting ready to take a bath and...I guess he came up behind me. The next thing I remember is waking up here."

"How could he get a needle into your vein?" Jerry asked in an accusatory tone.

"I don't know how he did it." Becky glanced at me, her eyes wide.

I put my hand on her shoulder. "Whatever happened the doctors will know—maybe he used chloroform."

"That outdated drug?" Jerry scoffed. "Now tell me the truth, Becky. Did you do this to yourself?"

"No, Jerry. I heard him come in."

"He has a key?"

"Yes. We'd been living together before we went up to Boston."

"So if you heard him come in why didn't you call the police?"

"There wasn't time. One second I was standing in the bathroom ready to get in the tub, and in the next I woke up here. You have to believe me."

"Maybe he knocked her out," I said, staring at Jerry. "The doctors can check for a bump on the back of her head. And if she did this to herself, where is the tubing and the needle?"

Jerry softened his hard look. "You're right. There was no syringe."

"I'm just glad you're all right," Valerie said, taking hold of Becky's hand.

"All he cared about was hurting me," Becky said, turning her head away.

I turned to Jerry, our eyes meeting over the bed. "Do you believe me now?"

He didn't answer, his gaze sliding away as a frown appeared between his brows.

A few moments later the doctor arrived to shoo us all out. "This woman nearly died and needs to rest," he said sternly. "You can all come back tomorrow during visiting hours."

"When will she be released?" Valerie asked.

"Two to three days." He checked the drip and turned to the machine beeping next to her.

Not much bedside manner, but it was obvious he cared about his patient.

Valerie rode the elevator down with us. "She's coming home to stay with me," she said decisively, her eyes on mine. "I'm not letting her out of my sight until that bastard is apprehended."

"About that," Jerry said, pulling out a small notebook. "What can you tell me about him? Name first, please."

By the time we left the hospital Jerry had Jacob's full name, a description, and my added details of approximately where he lived in Boston. Once we were alone in the cruiser he turned to me. "Jesus, Summer. This kind of thing shouldn't happen. It reminds of what happened to you last year."

My mind went to the man who roofied me. If Jerry hadn't arrived when he did, Jim Salazar would have raped me. I gazed at him, remembering how he'd spent the night in a chair next to my bed and helped me to the bathroom to throw-up. My heart softened as his dark eyes met mine. "You saved me."

He turned away. "It's what cops do."

"Really? I have a hard time imagining another cop doing what you did."

"Yes, well." He shook his head, running his hand across his unshaven chin.

It was then I noticed his scruffy beard and how tired he seemed. I hoped to hell he wasn't going through another breakdown. "Are you okay?"

"I will be once we talk, Summer. This last couple of weeks has been hard."

"How is your mom doing?"

"I'd rather not talk about her. But I will say that I'm off the hook for her care. I'm finally figuring out what you've said all along; she doesn't want me to grow up."

"Or she wants it to be on her terms."

"Yes, that too." He turned the key, brought the cruiser to life and put it into gear. We didn't talk again until he pulled up in front of my house. "See you tomorrow night?"

"Is tomorrow really Friday?"

Jerry smiled for the first time. "I see it's been a long week for you too." He gave me a quick kiss on my cheek before I got out.

CHAPTER TWENTY

By the time five o'clock rolled around I was nervous as a mouse being pursued by a cat. Jerry would be arriving in a half hour, I had yet to get home from Tarot and Tea, and I had nothing planned for food. But then I remembered I'd only invited him for wine. I did want to change my clothes and put on some lipstick at least. I was almost glad for the disaster with Becky, since it had broken down some of the tension between us. And knowing that she would be fine was another relief. I closed up and ran through pouring rain toward my car, trying not to slip on the slushy wet leaves underfoot.

I pulled my closet apart searching for the sage sweater I wanted to wear. After I found it, I pulled on my jeans, sucking in my breath to zip them up. Kicking away the pile of clothes, I closed the door on the mess.

The tightness of the jeans made it hard to breathe, but I dismissed the thought of all the scones and clotted cream I'd eaten in Scotland. I ignored the pressure around my stomach, and filled in my lips with a color called *luscious*, a red that Jerry liked, and then added silver hoop earrings to my ears.

What am I doing? I asked myself, staring into the mirror at the flushed and nervous girl who gazed back at me. I sighed and shrugged. I had to admit I loved him, and being attractive to him was important to me. But how to go from having an affair with a ghost, to him moving back in, was a question I had yet to answer. Not to mention his tangled relationship with his mother. Until that was completely settled, there could be no *us*.

Instead of knocking he used his key to enter my house, the sheepish grin and shrug his way of explaining it. "Sorry—force of habit."

I laughed and poured the already opened wine. "Can you bring the crackers and cheese to the living room?" I asked, grabbing both glasses.

We settled in front of the fire I'd made earlier, Cutty making a beeline for Jerry's lap. "Hello, little guy—did you miss me?"

I wriggled around trying to loosen the waistband of my jeans, finally turning away from Jerry to undo the top snap. "Did you hear anything today about Becky or Jacob?" I asked, taking in a deep breath.

"Actually, I have a lead on Jacob. I have cops staking out his place. If and when he comes out of there, he'll be picked up."

"He'll have to come out eventually."

Jerry nodded, taking a small sip. "And Becky did have a bump on the back of her head. He hit her a good one before he shot that poison into her veins."

"Ugh. That's just disgusting. Did Valerie tell you that?"

"She called this morning to give me some more details about Jacob. He's a real piece of work."
"I can't see Becky falling for him."

"Maybe he's a warlock."

I swiveled quickly to see the quirk of humor at the corner of his mouth. "What do you really think the attraction is, or was?"

He gave a one-shouldered shrug and put his glass on the table. "Old boyfriend, old connections—first love. It all adds up. It's hard to let go of fantasies like that."

"But Becky is so sensible and down to earth."

"That's probably the main reason she went for it. She was primed."

I thought about that. Had I been primed for Owen? I'd had that dream or vision early on—and after that...

"What happened to you in Scotland, Summer?" Jerry asked, as though reading my mind.

I struggled for words, finally saying, "The guy who killed Finlay...he and I were married in a past life."

Jerry's eyebrows pulled together. "You talked to this ghost?"

I nodded, taking a big gulp from my glass. "He was hanging around Ian's house, you know, the driver I told you about."

"And...he and you...what?"

"We took a trip up to the ruins—Ardvreck Castle? The place was built by Clan Macleod and later taken over by Clan Mackenzie. As you know, Finlay is a Macleod.

215

Owen is, or was, a Mackenzie. Finlay stole me and our two children away from Owen, and consequently Owen killed him."

"Whoa..." He picked up his glass and took a big swig. "That's definitely grounds for murder in my book."

"I agree, but when I ran all this by Finlay the other night, he went ballistic."

"Finlay...the ghost here in the graveyard?"

I nodded. "I told him what Owen said, and also told him he was in the wrong grave. That grave belongs to his son, not him. Finlay died in Scotland."

"How was he killed?"

I chuckled. "Owen cut his head off with a claymore sword."

Jerry just stared at me. "And you think this is funny?"

"It is if you're aware of what Finlay did. And after Finlay was killed, someone from Clan Macleod took revenge on Owen by torturing him. At least Finlay died immediately." I tried hard to hide the tears that welled.

"This really got to you, didn't it?"

"It did, especially because of meeting this Owen Mackenzie."

"What kind of past life did you dream about—was it rough and tumble or genteel, or what?"

"We lived in a large stone house with other members of his family. We had a room with a fireplace. I was always cold. We had a little girl and a boy. He hunted and fought with the other clans. I was aware of danger around every corner."

"Better in this timeline?" he asked softly.

"Better now," I agreed, looking away.

"So, tell me Summer. Are we getting back together or should I be looking elsewhere?"

Again, the glint of humor in his eyes. "You're welcome to look elsewhere, Jerry, but I doubt you'll find as fine a woman."

"I'm well aware of that, Ms. McCloud. What I'm asking is—"

My phone rang and I jumped up to answer it. "Becky? What's happening?"

I hung up the phone after she told me her news, turning to Jerry. "They caught the bastard. You're wanted at the station."

Jerry let out a long sigh and rose from the couch. "Bad timing," he muttered, getting his jacket. "Rain check?"

I nodded. He gave me a quick peck on the lips and then he was gone, the roar of his motorcycle diminishing as he headed toward the station. I sat on the couch and finished my wine, thinking about our conversation and what I hadn't revealed. Did I have the nerve to tell him all of it? I picked up his glass and drained it too. After that I stripped off my jeans and hurled them into the corner of my closet, vowing to lose the weight I'd gained.

I was deeply asleep when I heard a bang, my eyes flying open in alarm. Finlay stood at the foot of my bed glaring at me, the fire poker in his hand. "Ye have ruined everything, lass. I am bein' kicked out of the place where

I've lived for, according to ye, two hundred year or more."

I sat up and pulled the blanket around my shoulders. "Who's kicking you out?"

"The other departed, who do ye think? They say I have nae right to this one. They've been after me for a while now, sayin' I was in the wrong place."

"But your son has moved on. What difference does it make?"

"They want me to gae hame."

"Maybe that's a good idea, Finlay. You'll be with your family from back then."

He shook his fist at me and raised the poker. "Ye will pay for this, ye gobbermouch, mark my words. I canna go back there now that I remember it...the ones I hurt will be after me!"

"Like Aine and Owen and Elsbeth?" I asked.

When he moved toward me, brandishing the poker, I scooted backward, nearly falling off the bed in my attempt to ward him off.

"Ye may be in a early grave along with 'em!" he shouted. His yell brought Cutty to life, hackles rising as he jumped up on the bed between us. When he began a frenzied barking, Finlay disappeared, the poker clattering to the floor.

Thanks, Cutty," I murmured, hugging the dog. I was shaking all over. Finlay could leave the graveyard and he was able to pick up my iron poker. He could have killed me.

I lay awake for a long time wondering if he'd show up again, but finally I fell into a shallow sleep.

"Summer, my love, where have you been?"

I stared into Jerry's eyes, and then took the fuzzy-haired baby from him. "Was he a good boy?" The baby gurgled, looking up at me with bright eyes.

"Of course he was a good boy—he's always a good boy, except when he's not." Jerry let out a laugh.

I woke with an intake of breath. A near death experience followed by a dream in which Jerry and I had a baby together? Was there some connection between these two events? My hands went to my flat lower belly. Maybe it was only my biological clock ticking away and trying to get my attention.

I sat there until dawn began to creep around the windows, my bedroom lightening incrementally until I heard the buzz of life begin outside. First it was the honk of a car, then two dogs barking, and after that traffic began to sift past, tires crunching across the dirt that had been thrown out to break up the ice. I rose and padded into the kitchen, my gaze going to the espresso machine. I missed Jerry.

CHAPTER TWENTY-ONE

A week had passed before I had a chance to ask Douglas about Finlay. It was ten o'clock when I cornered him away from the other customers. "Can you tell me how to get rid of a ghost who's bothering me?" I whispered.

As usual Douglas was his calm gentlemanly self, his forehead puckering as he thought. "Can I assume this is about the ghost you met in Scotland?"

How did he know about Owen? "No, this is about Finlay in the Ames graveyard. He arrived in my bedroom in the middle of the night holding one of my fireplace tools."

"Finlay—the one who sent you to Scotland? *He's* angry with you?"

"Apparently so. I found out he isn't who he thought he was, and I told him that his murderer had good reason for doing what he did."

"Ah. Yes, that could cause some consternation in the afterlife. What does he want?"

"I don't know. All he did was call me some name and brandish my poker. He's scary."

"A witch might be able to help you. Perhaps your friend Becky can whip up a spell or two."

"That's a great idea. She needs to get her mind off Jacob, and what he did to her...oh, sorry. Have you heard?"

Douglas nodded. "Not much slips by the clientele at the Victorian; I must confess that they are rampant gossips. I was sorry to hear of it."

I had to laugh. "They caught Jacob."

Douglas nodded as though he was aware of that too. "Give Becky a call. You should at least have a spell of protection around your cottage." He patted me on the shoulder in a fatherly way and then headed toward Mrs. Browning.

Since everyone seemed content to browse, I took the opportunity to grab my cell, and punched in Becky's numbers. "How are you doing?" I asked.

"Summer, do you know of a rental or place I could stay? I can't live with mom on a long term basis, and I won't ever step foot into that apartment again."

I suddenly remembered the empty apartment over the shop. It hadn't been used since my mother's twin sister and my father had hidden up there. I was sure it needed major energy clearing after...I turned my mind away from the awful events of that summer, trying not to shudder. "How would you feel about the apartment over Tarot and Tea? It needs to be saged and cleaned, but it's certainly bigger than your tiny apartment."

"That's a perfect idea! Are you sure you don't need it for storage?"

"I might use the inside stairs for boxes from time to time, but other than that, no. And it has an outside entrance."

"How much would you charge?"

"Let me think on that. Maybe we could work out a trade of some kind. On another subject—do you know any spells to keep Finlay's ghost from harassing me?"

"Harassing—why? You just went on an overseas trip specifically for him."

"And what I found out didn't suit him."

Becky laughed. "I have a couple of binding spells I could combine with protection. Did he actually come into your house?"

"Yes, and he's capable of picking up heavy objects. He threatened me with a poker."

"Oh, this isn't good. A ghost that behaves like this is—"

"Is what?"

"He's dangerous, Summer. I've only seen this behavior one other time."

"And how did it end?"

There was a pause and then she said, "Not well, not well at all."

"I've got to go," I said when I heard my shop phone ring. "Let me know when you want to move in. As soon as I have a chance I'll air the place out and put some crystals around."

"Thanks so much. This is an enormous relief."

I closed out the call and rushed across the store to my desk.

"Summer? This is Jerry."

As if I wouldn't recognize his voice. "What's up?"

"I just wanted to let you know that Jacob Sells will be arraigned early next year. And the prosecution has your name on their witness list."

"Me? Why?"

"Because you can attest to Becky's state of mind, and she showed you her bruises. The guy is as slippery as an eel."

"Will I have to testify?"

"Maybe. But since you're only a hearsay witness they may just take your statement. How are you doing? Someone told me you had a haunting the other night."

The way news traveled in Ames was nothing short of amazing. Who had I even told besides Douglas, and... I looked around the store, noticing that Mrs. Browning was gone, and then I remembered seeing her talking to Valerie. One of them must have called Jerry. "Finlay threatened me with a fireplace poker." I let out a nervous laugh.

"What? That is not at all funny. You either need to let me stay with you, or I'll put a detail on your house at night." He paused to take in breath. "Well? What's it going to be?"

"Jerry, I...I don't think it's serious enough for that—and how will you explain to one of the officers that they are there to prevent a ghost from getting in? And Finlay doesn't use the door."

"That clinches it. I'll be there tonight." Before I could argue he'd hung up.

Jerry was in my cottage when I arrived home at five-thirty. I was glad to see him, but also not ready to talk about Owen and the parts of my trip I'd held back. He'd made a fire and lounged on the couch in front of it with a beer in his hand, Cutty curled up beside him.

He rose when I came through the door. "I'm sorry if you don't want me here, but the idea of a ghost threatening you was a bit much. I've put my things in the guest room."

I smiled and took my coat off, hanging it in the closet by the door. "I'm glad you're here, Jerry. I was really freaked out about it. I couldn't believe that frail-seeming ghost was able to heft a fire poker!"

"I don't get what is going on in this town...how many people walking down the street are ghosts? Is Ames just an anomaly, or are other towns like this?"

I shrugged. "It does seem odd, I have to admit. Douglas said Finlay could be dangerous."

"Haven't we already established that?" He sat on the couch again. "How do you feel about what I told you earlier about being a witness against Jacob Sells?"

"Not great, but if it helps put him behind bars, I'm willing to do it."

"From what we've found out the guy has been arrested numerous times, but always manages to avoid being charged. He preys on women, gets them addicted and takes their money."

"Ugh! What a bastard. Becky's moving in above the shop."

"I didn't think she'd want to go back to where she nearly died. Have you been up there since--?"

"Since you had to save me from my father and Mom's sister? Not really. It's going to need cleaning and sageing and maybe some crystals."

Jerry laughed. "You and your magical solutions to what is merely a memory."

"A memory? That place has bad juju, Jerry. My mother's creepy sister and my homicidal father lived up there for several months. You don't think they left bad energy behind?"

"I don't think of energy that way. But I'll come by if you need some help with it."

"There isn't much to do. I'd be better off having someone like Becky help me. She feels energy."

"How about just opening the windows?"

"Bad energy lurks in corners and sticks to stuff."

Jerry smirked. "If you say so." He took a sip of beer and grabbed my hand from where I stood in front of the fire. "Sit down. We need to have a talk."

"Isn't that what we're doing?" I pulled away and headed toward the kitchen, my mind recoiling at the idea of revisiting the topics we'd begun the last time we'd been together. "I have to make some food if we're going to have dinner." I felt Jerry's eyes on my back as I moved around the kitchen.

A moment later he was beside me. "Why are you avoiding me?"

I met his dark eyes, guilt surfacing. "I'm not. I just need to—"

Jerry grabbed me and pulled me close. "Do you still love me?"

A straight forward enough question. "I love you, Jerry, but—" I twisted away and opened the refrigerator, perusing the shelves without seeing what was there.

"But my mother, and your trip, the ghost, your work, Becky's problems—what else is between us right now?" He let out a humorless laugh. "Something is definitely going on with you, and I want to know what it is."

"I can't talk about it right now," I said with my back turned.

I heard him sigh and then the clunk of his bottle on the butcher block. "I've been meaning to—"

When my phone rang I hurried to where I'd left it on the coffee table. "Hi Agnes. What's up?"

"Is Jerry there?"

"Yes, why?"

"Jacob was released a little while ago. It seems there was something illegal about what the cops did—maybe they didn't read him his rights? Sam wants to talk to Jerry."

"Sam for you," I said, holding the phone out.

His mumbled conversation went on for a minute or two before he ended the call and handed the phone back. "Where is Becky?" he asked.

"At her mom's, I think."

"I need to warn her—Jacob is out."

Jerry was putting on his jacket when I came to my senses. "Maybe you should bring her here for the night. At least she'll have a cop's protection."

He turned. "Good idea. Can I borrow your car? That way I can head over to Valerie's and pick her up."

"Sure." I found the keys in my purse and tossed them. He caught them neatly in his right hand. "I'll make dinner for the three of us while you're gone."

By the time I heard the sound of my car tires crunching across the gravel in the driveway I'd fried up some chicken, tossed a salad and heated up some left over sweet potatoes. The food was waiting on the butcher block. Becky came in first, her face chalk white. Jerry followed, his expression grim.

He put her bag down and closed the door and locked it. "The bastard has already called and threatened," Jerry said, sliding the deadbolt across.

I moved to give Becky a hug. "I'm so glad you're here." She was shivering. "Do you want to take a hot shower before we eat? It'll warm you up."

Becky nodded gratefully. Jerry handed her the bag and we both watched her walk unsteadily toward my bedroom.

"I'm glad you suggested this," Jerry said, following me into the kitchen. "That woman has been traumatized enough."

"Who would have thought the guy would be so brazen?"

"Drug addicts are a peculiar bunch," Jerry muttered, pulling a piece of crispy chicken skin off and popping it into his mouth.

"What happens now?"

"He's been cut loose. Until he pulls some other stunt our hands are tied."

Once Becky had showered and changed into sweats and a long sleeved T-shirt, we had dinner, the three of us sitting around the kitchen table in near silence.

"Thank you," Becky said at one point. "I hope he doesn't think I'm at mom's."

"I have a black and white patrolling her house," Jerry assured her. "You can relax now."

After dinner Becky helped me clean up the kitchen while Jerry put the food away. Once we'd finished she turned to me. "If you don't mind I think I'll head to bed. I'm still feeling the effects of the overdose."

"And the drugs they gave you afterward," I reminded her.

"Where should I sleep?"

I suddenly realized that the guest bedroom had been allocated to Jerry. When I turned, his eyes met mine. "I'll sleep on the couch," he said. "That way I'll be in the perfect position to ward off the ghost."

"I'm sorry," Becky said.

"Don't be silly. Jerry has slept on my couch before-- it's as comfortable as a bed. And I'd feel better if he was out here anyway."

"Is it Finlay?"

I nodded. "We can talk about it tomorrow. You need to get a good night's rest."

Jerry headed into the guest room and got his bag. "It's all yours," he said, gesturing as he exited.

When the door closed behind her we looked at each other. "Are you sure you don't mind?"

Jerry scoffed and shook his head, placing his bag on a chair. "As long as you don't mind me using your bathroom. Can I shower?"

"Of course." I followed him into the bedroom, feeling silly about the arrangements. We were acting like we didn't know each other, when in reality we'd been living together for months before...before his mother's accident and my trip to Scotland...and Owen. I sat on the bed musing about it all and watching him pull his long-sleeved polo over his head.

His back was to me but his eyes met mine in the mirror in front of him. "This is kind of odd, wouldn't you say?"

"I was just thinking the same thing, but..."

"But there's still a wall between us. I can feel it. You built it, and until you feel like telling me what's going on, it's going to be there." He pulled off his jeans and slung them across a chair before heading into the bathroom in his boxers.

By the time he came out Cutty was on the bed and I'd closed the door to the living room. I had on pj's and was under the covers reading a book. Jerry retrieved a pair of boxers from his bag and let his towel drop, giving me a good long look at his naked butt before he slipped them on. A flush rose into my cheeks as I tried to focus on the page I was reading.

"What do you say?"

I looked up at him innocently. "What do I say about what?"

"Shall I bunk in here with you or stay out there. Didn't you say the ghost came into your bedroom?"

His expression betrayed nothing but exemplary cop behavior. I scoffed and put my book down. "Can you be good?"

He frowned. "What does that mean? Are you asking me not to try anything?"

I nodded, trying to hide my smile.

"I won't try anything unless you initiate it. Is that okay by you?"

"Yes."

He slid into his side of the bed, snuggling under the covers. I turned out the light on my side and slid down, my leg touching his. I pulled it away, but not before a tingle climbed up my thigh.

I was having a familiar dream of being with Jerry, our deep kisses making me long for more. His warm hands wandered under my T-shirt across my breasts, his mouth exploring my collarbone when I suddenly realized that this was no dream. "Hey!" I said, my eyes flying open. "What are you doing?"

It was very dark in the room and I could barely make out his features. But I could hear his elevated breathing, and I could feel... "Jerry, stop!"

His hands stopped moving and I heard the rustle of the bedclothes as he moved back. "What's wrong?"

"Didn't we have an agreement about this?"

"You're the one who started it, Summer. I was peacefully sleeping when you ran your fingers across my chest and kissed the back of my neck. You pressed your body against my back. What did you expect?"

I turned on the light. "I did not."

He rubbed his eyes, shielding them from the brightness. "Yes, Summer, you did."

I sat up and leaned against the headboard, trying to remember my dream. I couldn't remember the beginning. "But I was asleep."

"And how exactly was I supposed to know that?"

"I don't know. I'm sorry."

"I'm not." He pulled himself up and leaned next to me. "Your subconscious obviously wants my body," he murmured, gazing at me with his bedroom eyes.

He was right. My body longed for him, but we had to talk first. And after he heard what I had to say...

"Jesus, Summer. What in hell is going on with you?"

"Do you really want to get into this now? It's nearly two o'clock in the morning."

Jerry crossed him arms over his chest and frowned. I heard a whimper, my gaze going to Cutty who had found a pile of my discarded clothes to use as a bed. "Poor Cutty," I said.

"What about poor Jerry? You're torturing me. Is this some sort of punishment for how I was before you left for Scotland? I've thought long and hard about all that-- ask Sam--he'll tell you. The poor guy had to listen to me bitch and moan, trying to figure this shit out. You have no idea how hard it's been."

"And your conclusions were?"

"I already told you. My mother is a manipulative bitch who wants to control my life. I can't turn my back on her completely, but I'm keeping her at arm's length now." He stared at me, his eyes narrowing. "Now it's your turn."

"If I tell you, Jerry, you'll walk out of here and I'll probably never see you again."

"The only thing that could make me do that is if you fell in love with another guy." When I didn't answer his eyes widened. "That's it, isn't it? You fell for some Scottish dude. Why didn't you tell me instead of letting me make a fool of myself!" he shouted, jumping out of bed. He was naked, and I tried hard not to look at his body.

I shushed him, my gaze going to the wall between my bedroom and the guest room. "That isn't it."

He glared at me. "Then what?"

"I had a past life experience with a ghost."

"A past life...what? You said something about this earlier, but—"

"I met a ghost who was my husband in a previous life, Jerry."

"You told me that earlier, but...I guess the full implication didn't register." He shook his head, running his fingers through his thick hair. "I'm trying really hard not to lose it here, Summer. Please explain exactly what went on."

"Like I told you, his name was Owen Mackenzie. We were together in the 1700's. We had two children, a boy and a girl. He's the one who killed Finlay."

"Yeah, you mentioned this before. But are you saying you traveled backward in time like the Outlander chick?"

I shook my head. "He was hanging around waiting for me. He couldn't move on until..." I began to cry.

"What the hell, Summer? What happened between you? Was he real, I mean corporeal?"

"Yes, Jerry. I spent one night with him and then he was gone."

Jerry's stony gaze remained on my face for several very long moments. "So you're telling me that you had sex with him. And where did this happen—in some vision in the past, or in the present? Were you *you* in this scenario?"

I tried not to see the shock and sadness on Jerry's face. "He took me to this old falling-down one room cottage not too far from the ruins...said it belonged to him. But when we got inside it was fully furnished. In the morning I woke up alone on a bare straw mattress covered in an ancient and filthy quilt. The floors were dirt and there were cobwebs everywhere."

Jerry frowned in disbelief. "You traveled into the past together and had a night of sex?"

I stared at my drawn up knees. My throat closed up, a lump lodging itself there. When I didn't answer Jerry let out his held breath and stared at the floor.

When he looked up again there were tears in his eyes. "You loved this guy. You made love with him."

I nodded, my tears coming faster. "It had nothing to do with you, with us. I got caught up in the past. It was...I don't know how to describe it...like a dream."

Jerry sat on the bed, his head in his hands. "I don't know how to react. I feel betrayed, but I also feel...I don't know...kind of shaken that something like this could even happen. Do you still love him?"

I shook my head and wiped away my tears. "How can I love a man who doesn't exist anymore? I did love him in a past life, and I loved him when we were together, but—"

"You loved him when you were together. What was the sex like, Summer? It must have been pretty awesome for you to--"

"Jerry, he was my husband in a past life! Yes, I felt for him, but he's gone now. I can barely remember what he looked like!"

"He's gone for good?"

"Yes."

"How do you know?"

"Because he told me so before he disappeared the last time. He was waiting to say goodbye...that's why we got together."

"Jesus. Did you think of me at all when this was going on?"

"I did, but I was so caught up in the past that I couldn't feel bad about what happened. It was like I wasn't in this reality."

"When I called you, had you already...?"

"Yes."

He shook his head, his eyes clouding. "I knew those dreams meant something. They were too vivid." He stared at me. "Long reddish-brown hair, blue eyes. The guy was big. Is that him?"

I nodded, trying very hard not to picture Owen.

Jerry shivered and slipped under the covers. "I'm going to need to process this. I'm sure I'll have more questions, but right now I'm overwhelmed. I need to sleep."

I placed a hand on his arm. "You don't hate me?"

He turned his head on the pillow. "I could never hate you, Summer. But it's a lot to take in. I knew something happened on your trip, but this..." He shook his head, an expression of misery on his features. "Can you turn out the light?"

I lay awake listening to Jerry's labored breathing. I knew he wasn't sleeping, and I could tell he was trying hard not to cry. I wanted to comfort him, wanted to put my arms around him and tell him I loved him, but I knew it wouldn't help. All my feelings for him rose to the surface of my mind. What had I done?

CHAPTER TWENTY-TWO

Jerry was gone in the morning, his bag as well. My stomach clenched, adrenaline propelling me out of bed. Cutty bounced out behind me, his tail wagging. After sliding my feet into my mukluks that served for winter slippers, I headed into the kitchen. The espresso machine was still there, a note taped to its silver metal side.

I need time to think. I'm sending a rookie over to sleep on your couch tonight. I'll be in touch. J

I heard the guest bedroom door open, Becky appearing in a long nightgown, hair tangled around her pale face. She smiled and came into the kitchen.

"What do you think of this?" I asked, holding out the note.

Becky read it through, her eyebrows scrunched. "I think I need context," she said, looking up.

"I told him about Owen last night."

"Ah. Yes, I would imagine he'd need a day or two to process *that.*"

'So I shouldn't be worried?"

"That must have been a lot for someone like Jerry to accept. How did he react?"

"Pretty calm, considering. He was kind of teary-eyed."

"I'd say that's a promising sign. How about you? How do you feel about him? Did he sleep with you in the bedroom?"

I scoffed and began making my espresso. "Yes, and apparently I initiated sex in my sleep."

Becky laughed. "You must miss him then."

"I do. We didn't get very far before I woke up."

"Had you already told him about Owen?"

"No. That's when I told him."

Becky stared out the window. "It's going to be a nice day," she said pointing to the blue sky.

"I followed her gaze. I hadn't even noticed. "Becky, can you cast a spell or two to keep Finlay out of here?"

She brought her attention back to me, pulling her hands into the sleeves of her long flannel nightgown. "I can do a binding spell to keep him away. If you have a bunch of crystals I can also do a protection spell. Maybe I should do one to keep him in the graveyard."

"No. He needs to go home to Scotland." I finished making espresso. "Would you like a coffee?"

"Do you have some tea?"

I nodded and turned the gas on, placing the teakettle over the flame. "I'm sorry it's so cold in here. I'll make a fire. You can turn up the thermostat, but it's kind of temperamental." I went to the fireplace and placed the paper, kindling and logs in the way my mother had taught me when I was a little girl. I lit the paper and stepped back, glad when the kindling began to burn. It was pine and very dry. By the time Becky had her tea in hand it was burning merrily and the small living room had warmed up.

With Becky planning to do her witchy stuff I had an excuse to call Jerry. I had to tell him not to send the rookie over, didn't I? We sipped our morning drinks in companionable silence, both of us watching the flames.

Once my cup was empty I rose from the couch and headed to the kitchen. "Do you want breakfast?"

She waved her hand in the air. "Don't go to any special trouble for me."

"It's no trouble. I was planning to make eggs and spinach."

"That sounds delicious. Do you have time to help me get some things from the apartment? I thought I'd begin moving in above Tarot and Tea today, if that's okay."

"I'd be happy to. It's early yet, and if we get a move on we can do it before I open the store." I looked at her thin face, the hollows beneath her eyes. "But honestly, I think you should stay here for a couple of days; I don't like to think of you alone right now."

"Let's see how it feels up there. If we can clear the energy, and I put some binding spells on Jacob, I should be fine. Besides, he won't know where I am. I promised Mom I'd call her this morning," she finished, heading to the bedroom. I heard her talking as I cooked. When she came out again she was dressed, her hair braided. "Mom said all was quiet last night."

I carried plates to the table. "That's good to hear. Breakfast is served."

After breakfast was over and I'd cleaned up I called Jerry. "I can't talk now, Summer," he said before I had the chance to say hello.

"I only called to let you know that I don't need the protection tonight. Becky is doing some binding spells to keep Finlay away."

"Are you sure?" Jerry sounded skeptical.

"I trust her, Jerry—she's a proper witch."

"Okay. I'll let Evans know."

I was about to say something else when he hung up. Okay, nothing to worry about. He either needed time, or there was something going on at the station. A niggle of doubt twined its way from my stomach to my throat, but I ignored it, turning to Becky who watched me with a frown.

"What's that about?" she asked.

"I just told him I wouldn't need the protection detail tonight."

"I actually meant the faraway expression on your face and the several emotions I saw flit across. You looked guilty, ashamed, sad and worried all at the same time."

"That about sums it up. Jerry feels bad, Becky, and it's my fault."

She pressed her lips together, scoffing. "You two have weathered worse. From what you told me he didn't fly off the handle. And now he's taking care of himself."

"That's true. Normally he would have stormed out of here in the middle of the night, furious. I guess I should give him credit."

Becky smiled. "Maybe he's growing up."

"He did say he's been dealing with his mother. And I guess he's been talking a lot with Sam."

"That's good. It means he's finally opening up. Jerry…" She gazed at me.

"Jerry what?"

"Jerry has some psychological problems. Maybe this thing with Owen will help him face what's going on."

"If you mean the stuff with his mom, yeah. He said he's dealing with it."

Becky nodded, but I had the sense there was more to her pronouncement.

Shortly after this conversation we put on heavy coats, climbed into my car and headed to her apartment.

"When can you cast the spells to keep Finlay out?" I asked as we neared the complex.

"I already did."

"What? When?"

Becky laughed. "It isn't such a big deal, Summer. I did it while you were on the phone and staring into space. Finlay will not be able to get anywhere near you now."

"But can I still go to the graveyard?"

"Yes. But why would you?"

"I feel bad about what I said and how I said it."

"Summer, what has got into you? First Jerry, and now Finlay, who threatened you with a poker? You don't seem like yourself."

When I swiveled to look at her the car swerved toward the curb. I twisted the wheel and brought us back onto the road. "What are you saying?"

"I've always known you to be a strong minded woman, not a doormat. You had an awesome and mind-boggling experience in Scotland, and also found out exactly what happened to Finlay. If Finlay can't take it, why is it your responsibility to assuage his feelings? He was a bastard during his life. And same goes for Jerry. He has to see you for who you really are if your relationship is going to continue."

"You should have been a therapist. And you're right. I haven't been myself since Owen. He haunts me, Becky. I don't know if he's really haunting me, but I can't get him out of my mind."

"Okay—that calls for another spell, Summer. You've been caught in his aura. Once we get to Tarot and Tea you need to collect as many crystals as you can. You can lie on the floor and I'll place them around you before I say the words. You need to be free of Owen."

"But what if I don't want to be?" I asked in a small voice.

"You're trapped in an obsession about a man long dead. Does that seem healthy to you? And what about Jerry? Ask yourself if you still love him."

I stared at the road ahead, swerving again to avoid hitting a squirrel. It was only a minute before we reached her apartment. "I still love Jerry…I just don't know if—"

"If what? He's a living breathing man who loves you. Would you give that up for a ghost?"

I parked the car and the two of us got out and headed toward her apartment on the second floor. When we reached her door, it was wide open. "What the hell?" Becky muttered. She went ahead of me, her screech propelling me quickly after her. The place was empty. Becky turned to me, her face even whiter than before. "He took everything—my T.V., my computer, my grandmother's antique furniture—everything."

"Why would he want it?"

"Money for drugs." She hurried into the tiny kitchen, her mouth dropping open when she looked in the cupboards. "All my dishes and my flatware—my pots and pans?" Becky shook her head, tears filling her eyes. "Those dishes came from my grandmother too. They were old, from Scotland, and can't be replaced." I followed her out to the living room were she collapsed on the wall-to-wall carpeting. She burst into tears.

I sat next to her, placing an arm around her shoulders. "I am so sorry, Becky—but the good news is he can be arrested now for theft. And if it happens soon enough, you may get some of your stuff back."

She gazed at me, a slightly hopeful expression appearing on her face. "Do you think so? He must have a storage unit somewhere, and getting any real money for antiques is iffy without proving provenance. Do you have Jerry's number?"

I queued up his number and handed her my phone. She hit call and listened and then left a message. "He must be busy."

"Probably thought it was me calling and decided not to answer. He has your number in his phone, right?"

"I think so."

That question was answered a moment later when Becky's phone rang. She glanced at me before answering.

Becky told him the entire sad story while I checked in the closets for anything that might have been left behind. There was nothing but a few strewn papers that had been left on the floor.

"Is there any way you can find his storage unit or where he's stashed the stuff?" I heard her ask when I came back. "Maybe someone saw his truck when he took it all." She listened for another moment and then said, "Okay," before she handed me the phone. "He says to ask the neighbors if they saw anything last night. And the fact that he had a key doesn't look well for me. According to Jerry, I should have had the locks changed."

"You were in the hospital! Just because you gave him a key, excuses him from taking everything you own?"

"The law looks at things differently, Summer."

"That man needs to be put behind bars, and if Jerry and his band of merry men can't manage it, then you and I will have to stage a sting."

Becky laughed. "There's the woman I know and love. But how do you propose to do it?"

"We could trap him into giving himself away. He's never met me...maybe I could, you know, ask him for drugs or something."

"Too dangerous. The guy is seriously deranged. I don't want you ending up in the hospital—or worse," she added darkly.

I looked up at the clock on the wall, the only thing he'd left behind. "I've got to get to work. I can drop you at the bakery, or you can take a look at the apartment upstairs and see what you think of the place. I have some sage in the store."

"That sounds best. I'm not ready to face Mom. She's going to completely lose it when she finds out all of Grandma's stuff is gone."

I opened the store with just minutes to spare, ushering in Douglas and Mrs. Browning, my usual early birds. "What's the latest?" Douglas whispered as he went by. I glanced at Becky talking with Mrs. Browning. "Becky cast a binding spell to keep Finlay away."

His eyes crinkled at the corners. "Did Agnes invite you to her Christmas party?"

"Christmas party? I stared at him. "What's today's date?"

"You've lost track of time? Today is December first. The party is on the twenty-first...winter solstice."

Where had November gone? I wondered if I'd time-slipped or something. "What happened to Thanksgiving?"

"Was that the week you retrieved Becky from Boston?"

I counted backward but got nowhere. "Since my trip to Scotland a lot has happened around here. I'll call

Agnes after I've sorted things out for Becky. Becky's former boyfriend just stole everything she had."

Douglas's eyes darkened. "She should have cast a binding spell on him."

"Unfortunately she was in the hospital recovering from the overdose he forced on her."

Douglas stared into the shadows behind the bookcases. "He will come to justice," he intoned.

"I'm glad you think so, but I hope it happens soon. She's heartbroken after losing all her heirlooms."

When Becky came toward us I steered her to the staircase leading up to the apartment. "Go check it out. I'll be up after I find a stick of sage." While I was searching for the sage Mrs. Browning arrived at my shoulder. "That poor girl has been through enough," she said in an angry tone. "I have a mind to do something about that boy."

"Like what?"

"I have my ways." She smiled evilly and headed toward Douglas.

Once I had the sage in hand, I hurried upstairs, hoping no one would want to be checked out before I got back. Becky was wandering around with a thoughtful expression, looking at my mother's old furniture. "Can this stay?"

"Of course. The entire place is furnished."

"And I'm very glad it is."

"You may need a few odds and ends, like new sheets and towels, but my mother's twin sister, Vivienne, and my father, lived up here for months. There should be everything you need."

"The energy up here is really funky. Light that sage and let's clear it out."

I searched in the kitchen for matches and lit the stick, but when I heard someone call my name I handed it to her. "Make sure you sage the closet—I had a very bad experience in there."

"Bring up the crystals when you get a chance and I'll clear the ghost out of your aura."

I paused at the top of the stairs. "Are you sure, after what you just went through?"

"I'm fine now."

"If you say so," I said, heading down the stairs.

During the lunch hour I put the shut sign on the door and gathered crystals. When I reached the apartment Becky was sitting on the couch, gazing around with a pleased expression.

"Can you do the thingy now?"

Becky laughed. "Now that I've saged up here, yes." She took the crystals out of my hands. "Lie down." She pointed to the rug in front of the couch.

I did as she asked, watching her place the crystals at my head and feet and along my waist on either side. She placed one in the middle of my chest and one on my lower belly.

"Relax, Summer. I can't clear energy while you're fidgeting. You closed the shop, right? Forget about everything for a few minutes. Let your mind float. Now close your eyes."

I listened to her mumbled chant, feeling the energy around me shifting and changing. I saw Owen receding until he looked like a pixilated image. And then he was gone altogether. When Jerry came into my mind, a warm sensation moved up my spine. I suddenly longed for him, wishing I'd never gone to Scotland. If only...

"Stop thinking!" Becky ordered.

I let out a long sigh, my thoughts drifting away. I was nearly asleep when I heard Becky say, "It's done. He won't be haunting you anymore."

"Thank you," I said sitting up. My head felt clear and light, until I heard the banging on my shop door. Becky and I exchanged a glance.

"Guess you'd better get back to work," she smiled.

It was nearly closing time when I heard Becky clattering down the stairs. "I love it up there. And the energy feels great now. I pulled the sheets off the bed and collected all the towels. I think I have enough money to buy myself a few things."

"I'm about to call Jerry and tell him to get on Jacob's trail ASAP."

"Don't, Summer. He made it clear he needed some time. Be mature enough to give it to him."

I snorted. "You're saying I have ulterior motives?"

She did a one-shoulder shrug, her eyebrows rising. "Do you?"

"Maybe," I said honestly. "What now? Do you want to stay here tonight, or stay at my house? I have a washing machine if you want the sheets and towels laundered."

"I'm going to stay with Mom tonight, if you don't mind giving me a lift. Even though I'm dreading it, I have to tell her what happened. And it's time I took over the bakery again. Don't worry, there will be binding spells everywhere. That creep will never get close to me again."

I smiled. "You helped me, Becky. I feel different since the crystal, whatever that was."

Becky grinned. "You should wash those crystals. They took on the dark energy. Part of you was hanging on to him."

"I could feel that, but I didn't know what to do. He was coming between Jerry and me."

"You do know that was you, right? Owen was gone. It was you keeping the memory--maybe to protect yourself? Maybe you're not quite ready to move forward with Jerry."

"I know I love him, but I'm sick of the on and off again thing we have going. Something about seeing the relationship I had with Owen, having two children with him, and knowing he was there for me...I want that with Jerry, but I don't think he can give it to me."

Becky smiled. "Both of you push each other away. Think on that for a while, and give him time to sort through his own feelings. You guys will figure it out."

I dropped Becky off at Valerie's house before heading home. I wasn't looking forward to being alone, but I ignored the hollow feeling in my belly. Cutty greeted me with his usual enthusiasm, dispelling some of my apprehension. With the spells in place I had nothing to worry about. It was Jerry's absence that was bothering me the most. But Becky's words of wisdom came back to me. I'd dropped a bombshell on the poor guy. I thought about how I would feel if he'd had an affair with a ghost—not good. With all our ups and downs we'd never been unfaithful to each other.

Once I'd poured a glass of wine and begun heating leftovers I called Agnes. After explaining all the latest news about Jerry and Becky, I settled in to hear what was happening with the baby and Sam, but instead of regaling me with the usual, she was oddly quiet. I finally asked what was wrong.

"Nothing's *wrong*, Summer. It's just that Jerry came by and told us his version of events, and since he and Sam are so close I invited him to our party…"

"And I'm not invited."

"I'm *sorry*! But Jerry specifically said if you were coming he'd have to bow out. He told us he's taking some time to think things through after what you told him. He seems to be doing better than I would have expected after hearing that you had an affair."

"It wasn't really an affair. I had one night with a ghost who disappeared immediately afterward…and we were married in a previous life."

"And that makes it okay."

"I can't help what happened. It was as surprising to me as anyone. Jerry was upset, but he did seem to understand."

"I don't see how anyone could understand; I certainly wouldn't be able to. How do you compete with a man that's dead? If you haven't noticed, Jerry has changed. He doesn't fly off the handle like he used to, and he's more thoughtful now."

"Well, actually, Agnes, I had noticed. I don't appreciate you acting like you know him better than I do."

There was a moment of silence. "He spent a lot of time with us while you were in Scotland, and lately too."

"I would say that's great, except you seem to have turned on me. Do you consider me a pariah now?"

"No, of course not. I guess I've been feeling sorry for Jerry. He seems so dejected."

Guilt rolled through me. "But he's the one who needed time."

"I hope the two of you can make a go of it. I'd hate to see you break up for good, especially after what Jerry's been thinking about. He…" There was a wail and then Agnes said, "Got to go."

"He what?" I asked the dead phone, throwing it across the room. It hit the wall and I heard a crack. I stared down at Cutty who watched me with bright eyes. My stomach had suddenly turned into a mass of knots.

CHAPTER TWENTY-THREE

It was the day of winter solstice when Becky called me with news that I should have gotten from Jerry. "Jacob's dead. Jerry and his band of merry men, as you call them, found his body in that horrible place in Boston."

"Oh my gosh! I don't know what to say. I guess that's good news."

"Now all we have to do is find out where he stashed my stuff."

"Did you ask your neighbors if they saw anything?"

"The woman next door said she saw the truck drive up and just assumed I was moving. She said there were two guys who loaded my stuff on and one of them had a shaved head. That was Jacob and probably his friend Eron. The truck was one from U-Haul. People move in and out of that apartment complex all the time."

"How did he die?"

"How do you think? An overdose, of course. He must have sold something of mine to get enough of that crap in his veins to kill him."

"Gross. The entire thing is so creepy. What about the others who lived there? Did Jerry arrest them?"

"Oddly, Jacob was alone when they found him. And according to the super, the others had vacated the week before. He'd been dead for at least two days."

I thought of Mrs. Browning and her angry pronouncement. Had she been involved in Jacob's death? Couldn't be. "There's got to be some evidence or a clue as to where he stored your stuff...like a key or something? I'm sure they'll find it."

"I hope so."

"What about his family? Did someone contact them?"

"I'm leaving that up to Jerry. I want nothing more to do with it. And besides, he told me his parents had basically disowned him. For good reason, if you ask me."

"How are you feeling about it all, Becky? He was your first love."

There was a moment of silence before she said, "He killed any love I still had for him when he forced that needle into my arm the first time. I have no feelings at all, aside from relief."

"Are you going to Agnes's party tonight?"

"I am. What time will you be there?"

I let out a sigh. "I wasn't invited."

"What! Why?"

"Because Jerry doesn't want to see my face? Honestly, I don't know."

"But Agnes is one of your best friends!"

"*Was* one of my best friends. She chose Jerry over me."

"Don't let it bother you. How about I ditch the party and you and I can celebrate?"

"I couldn't ask you to do that, Becky. And besides, I need you to spy for me."

Becky chuckled. "Jerry, I assume?"

"Yes. I've heard nothing from him since the night I told him about Owen. I want to know if he's with someone else."

She scoffed. "He's not with anyone else—that man loves you."

"Everyone keeps telling me that, but if it's true then why hasn't he called?"

"It was a lot to take in, Summer. He needs some time. And he's had his hands full with Jacob's case and all the rest of the bizarre events that happen when the dark usurps the light."

I laughed. "You poetess, you."

"The first full moon coven at the Victorian is happening in a few days. Will you be there?"

"With bells on. Thanks for reminding me."

"I love you, Summer. You've been my mainstay during this terrible time. Don't despair when it comes to Jerry. I'll have my witch hat on tonight."

"Thanks, Becks."

"Did I hear that you won't be at my daughter's tonight?" Douglas asked once I got off the phone.

"She didn't invite me."

Douglas frowned. "I'll have to have a talk with her. Ever since the baby came she's been acting like a princess."

"It's only because of Jerry. He doesn't want to be around me right now."

"Is this still about what happened in Scotland? What is *wrong* with that young man! He needs to get his head—"

I held up my hand, surprised by his vehemence. "He needs time to work it through, and knowing Jerry, that will take a while."

"I'm sorry my daughter is going along with this silliness. She should have invited both of you and allowed the chips to fall where they might."

I grimaced. "I kind of think so too. But being alone tonight is probably good for me. How is little Sammy? I haven't seen him in a month!"

"He's growing like a weed…sitting up now. I'm shocked she hasn't reached out to you, Summer."

I waved my hand in the air like it was nothing, but I couldn't deny that I felt hurt. "Once Jerry decides he can handle seeing me, I'm sure things will get back to normal."

When Mrs. Browning arrived later I told her about Jacob, trying to gauge her reaction. She didn't seem at all surprised, a knowing smile hovering around her thin lips. "Couldn't happen to a nicer person," she said.

I stared at her, feeling a little chill.

When I left the store to drive home, the sky had gone from pale grey to charcoal, threatening clouds building to the north. Darkness rolled over Ames, making me wonder if we were in some kind of vortex of crappy weather. Tonight would be well below freezing, I was sure of it.

Despite my protestations to the contrary, I hated the idea of missing the party. It was winter solstice, a time to be with friends and offer up libations to the goddess. A second later my loneliness turned into anger at the world. Why did I have to suffer because Jerry couldn't cope with my past life experience? The ghost was long gone; his image had faded from my memory. Sometimes when I thought back on it, the entire experience seemed like an impossible dream. Had I imagined the whole thing? But I knew better.

A moment later I thought about my own feelings. This wasn't about Jerry. It was about me. I wanted a steady relationship, one I could count on. He must have made up his mind by now. Which meant that he'd probably decided to call it quits.

My car sputtered and died a half a mile from the cottage. "Well, I guess you decided to give up the ghost," I muttered, the irony of my whispered words making me chuckle. I'd been planning to take her in for weeks and hadn't yet had a chance. For a moment I wondered if my dark thoughts had caused her sudden demise.

Despite being chilled when I reached home, I was determined to take Cutty for a walk before dinner. As soon as I came through the door he was there, his leash in his mouth. I clipped it to his collar and closed the door behind us. He pulled me toward the back of the cottage, making a beeline toward the graveyard. "Why do you want to go there?"

I could have steered him in a different direction, but decided it was time to face my fears. Finlay hadn't been back since Becky had placed the binding spells, but still I wanted to talk with him and find out if he was still angry. *Not a good idea*, a little voice said, but I kept going anyway.

At the gate I unclipped the leash and headed through, Cutty on my heels. When I reached the grave I called out to him softly. "Finlay? Are you there?"

There was no answer. I grew cold waiting for him, and was about to turn away, when I heard a whispery voice say, "He's moved on."

I turned toward the sound, but all I could see was a pale shimmer. "Are you sure?"

"Yes…" the voice lengthened out the word, hissing before dissolving into the whistle of wind in the trees. I let out a sigh and headed toward the gate, part of me sorry that I would never speak to my relative again. But I was also glad he'd gone home where he belonged. I had a sudden image of Owen, Aine and Elsbeth going after him with clubs in their hands. "You brought it on yourself," I muttered.

After dinner I had my own solstice celebration, trying not to think about the party as I sipped champagne and threw a libation on the fire for the goddess. "Thank you," I whispered, glad for everything that had happened.

A few moments later I felt a great weight lifting from me—the last remnant of Owen I'd been holding onto. The fire spit and crackled, bringing my attention back. I watched the almost liquid movement of the flames, a metaphor for the capriciousness of life.

It was nearly midnight before I went to bed, glad for the time alone, and my own rituals of letting go and appreciation. Cutty and the cats were curled up on my bed by the time I banked the fire and headed into the bedroom. One last look out the window revealed a blanket of white, fitting for the longest night of the year. I snuggled under the covers with my animals close around me.

I woke later than I'd planned, unprepared for how cold the house had grown. Cutty was shivering, and I had no idea where the cats had gone. My down comforter and the addition of a wool blanket had allowed me to sleep in. I hurried to the thermostat before realizing that the power was off. Outside was a winter fairyland, a halo of pale sunlight just visible behind the thin layer of cloud. I made a fire and urged Cutty close, bringing his food dish so he could eat by the warmth. "No espresso," I muttered sadly.

I was still huddled there when my cell phone rang. At least the cell towers were still working. It was Becky.

"Is your electricity out? Tarot and Tea doesn't have power."

"The fireplace up there works, but I don't think there's wood."

"No wood. It's freezing! I hope the pipes don't burst!"

"Don't even say that. I have a generator somewhere, but my car isn't working. Can you walk over here? At least I have the fireplace."

"I'll be there as soon as I can."

It was nearly an hour before I heard stomping feet outside. I opened the door and laughed. "You look like an Eskimo." She was wearing the heaviest down coat I'd ever seen, the furred hood covering everything but her red-cheeked round face.

She pulled off her mittens and boots by the door and moved toward the fire. "It's three degrees out there."

"How did you find that out?"

She held out her new cell phone, showing me the local news on the screen. "Emergency crews are all over town trying to get the power back on." It was a few minutes before she was willing to remove her coat. "I'm worried about the bakery if the pipes burst."

"How was the party?"

"I was wondering how long it would take you to ask." She smiled and moved closer to the fire. "Jerry was alone and seemed somber. He hardly drank and he left early."

"So no woman with him. Did you talk to him?"

"Only about Jacob and my stuff. He found some evidence of a storage unit in some papers strewn across the apartment floor. I guess the place was a mess, with needles and paraphernalia everywhere." Becky shuddered. "As soon as the weather allows he's sending a crew to look into it."

"That's good news. I went to the graveyard last night and it seems that Finlay has moved on."

"Really? Maybe my binding spells sent him packing, so to speak."

"I think they did. How is Agnes?"

"She's great. The baby is adorable. When I asked her about not inviting you she got teary. I guess Douglas gave her a tongue-lashing. She said it was because of Jerry and Sam's friendship. She's worried that you're mad at her."

"I am mad at her."

"Well, it's the start of a new year—let it go."

"Easy for you to say."

"Is it? I've had my share of bad stuff this year too."

"But your best friend didn't turn her back on you."

Her steady gaze met mine. "A man I trusted and loved tried to kill me and then stole everything I owned."

"I'm sorry, Becks. I wasn't looking at it like that."

"And now he's dead."

I watched her eyes fill with tears. "You did still care for him."

She nodded and wiped her eyes with her sleeve. "I know I said I was over it, but it's hard to let go of how he was when we first met. I keep seeing the man I knew before. I always thought he would come out of this...whatever it was he was going through. But he didn't."

"Did I tell you that Owen tried to kill me?"

She turned to stare at me. "When did that happen?"

"The night before I left. I woke up with his hands around my throat. I think he hoped that if I died we could be together."

Becky stared into the flames. "Maybe that's why Jacob did what he did, but I doubt it." Her gaze met mine. "Do you think Jacob overdosed on purpose?"

"Accidents like that are often not really accidents, if you know what I mean. Maybe you can do some kind of ritual on coven night."

"That's a good idea—some kind of letting go. You can join me." She smiled.

"Is Agnes going?"

"I didn't ask."

The power came on soon after that conversation, both of us relieved. We put on our coats and boots and walked together through the snowy, deserted streets to Tarot and Tea. Once we'd checked and made sure that the pipes hadn't frozen we headed to the bakery. Valerie was there, her worried gaze on her daughter. "I think things are all right," Valerie said. "But you'd know better."

Becky headed into the back to check the faucets, coming out with a smile on her face a few minutes later. "Everything's fine."

Valerie hugged her. "I miss you," I heard her whisper.

Becky gave her mom a pat on the shoulder as she pulled away. "You say that now, but after a few more weeks we would have grated on each other's nerves."

The three of us left the bakery and headed toward Down and Dirty, the local coffee shop. Thankfully it was open. As we drank our lattes Valerie told us what she'd seen in her cards.

"I knew something very bad was going to happen to that boy. And I also knew he was going to hurt you. But by the time I read the cards it was too late."

"It's all over now," Becky said, trying to reassure her mother. "Do you have your cards with you? Maybe Summer would like a reading."

Before I could say, no, Valerie was gazing at me brightly, the worn deck in her hand. "Let's see what your future holds, Summer," she said, handing me the deck to shuffle.

I looked around the nearly empty coffee shop as I moved the cards in my hands. Jerry's face loomed up, his dark eyes sad. What would happen with us?

CHAPTER TWENTY-FOUR

It wasn't until I got home that the true meaning of the cards came to me. The Hanged Man upside down had been the centerpiece of the reading: suspended in time, something moving out of my life, stalling on a decision, acting selfishly. I interpreted it to mean that the ghosts had moved out, and as far as stalling, that could mean not being honest with Jerry about what I wanted from our relationship. The selfishness could be about Agnes and my refusal to forgive her.

And the second card wasn't any better. The Chariot reversed had several meanings I didn't want to see--loss of control and the idea that it would be better for me if I gave up control, and not to be afraid to let someone else have control. Jerry and I had compromised in the past, but many of our arguments had been related to this one issue. We were both stubborn.

The six of wands reversed was the card that represented the present: doubting myself, being punished, confidence down. What I wanted was steadiness, a relationship that I could count on, but in some dark corner of my mind I didn't think I deserved it.

And then the two of swords, which suggested that I was avoiding making a decision. The swords represented the pros and cons I needed to weigh. Also it indicated indecision and stalemate. Ugh. Wasn't it Jerry who had to make the decision? But I knew that until we were truly honest about what we wanted there was no way forward.

But it was the last card that really threw me. The reversed seven of wands pointed to the fact that I'd taken on too much and that I was feeling overwhelmed. I was trying to avoid conflict and feeling shaken and vulnerable. And I was feeling aggressive about protecting myself. I ticked through the reasons: Falling in love with Owen, Finlay's aggressive behavior, Becky and all her problems, Agnes and her support of Jerry, Jerry himself and his lack of contact with me. I was afraid to talk to Jerry, to tell him what I wanted.

I was crying now, and didn't know where to turn for comfort. I couldn't keep calling on Becky, who had her own set of problems, Agnes was out of the question, and Jerry...Jerry didn't love me anymore.

The next day I called the Honda dealer and had my car towed there to be repaired. When they called to tell me the entire engine had to be overhauled, I burst into tears. "I don't have the money for that," I sobbed into the phone.

"Maybe we can set up a payment plan," the man said gently. "Since you bought the car from us I'll ask the boss and see what we can do."

Once I was off the phone I dressed warmly and walked to Tarot and Tea. I had to get my head on straight. I had a business to run.

I was concentrated on my receipts when Douglas walked up to the desk. "Wanted to let you know I had a long talk with my daughter. She regrets her behavior."

"Thanks, Douglas, but it's okay. She's only trying to support Jerry."

Douglas frowned. "Are you coming to the full moon coven tonight?"

"My car's in the shop."

Douglas glanced behind him at Valerie. "Valerie will give you a ride, won't you Valerie?" he called out.

She came toward us, an expectant look on her face. "What's that?"

"Can you give Summer a ride tonight?"

She smiled. "Of course. Becky is going with me as well."

"I don't want you to go out of your way."

Valerie placed a hand on my shoulder, a look of sympathy on her face. "That Tarot reading got to you, didn't it? The cards are not set in stone, my dear. And many meanings can be gleaned, both positive and negative. What you need is to offer up your prayers to Aine, the moon goddess."

"Aine?"

"The Celtic moon goddess, dear. You must know about her."

I was suddenly plunged into the past. I shook myself and brought my mind back to the present. "My name was Aine in a past life," I finally managed to mutter.

"When you were with that handsome Scottish ghost?"

I let out an exasperated sigh. "If you mean, Owen, then yes." How did she know if he was handsome or not? I certainly hadn't mentioned it. Maybe I'd described him to Becky.

"I'll pick you up at nine o'clock."

"Thanks, I'll be ready." I turned back to the papers strewn across my desk.

I was waiting outside when Valerie's headlights wended their way down my street. When I climbed inside, the car was warm, the heater at full blast. "Thanks for picking me up."

Becky turned to face me. "I'm so glad you're coming tonight. I know this will help your mood."

"Is it that obvious?"

"Not to most people, but I know you."

"Things will begin to clear up after tonight," Valerie added, her eyes meeting mine in the rear view mirror. "Both for you and my daughter."

"Is that a premonition or just wishful thinking?"

"A bit of both," she answered, smiling.

The Victorian was lit up like a birthday cake. I could hear animated voices as we hurried to the front door.

Inside at least one hundred people milled about, many of whom I hadn't seen since the summer. Everyone seemed excited and happy to conduct our full moon ritual again without worrying about being hauled off to jail.

I looked around the ballroom, the enormous gilt mirrors from a bygone era, the black and white tiled floors, the decorative columns and wide French doors, that all lent elegance. Red velvet bows hung from the columns, sprigs of holly and pine arranged on the wide stone mantel. The enormous fireplace burned brightly, the sound of crackling wood echoing in the high-ceilinged room. I hadn't been here since Agnes and Sam's wedding in early spring.

"We aren't having it in here?" I asked Douglas who was directly inside the door, acting as greeter.

"No, no. We will go out onto the patio where we can commune with the goddess moon. She isn't visible yet."

I looked around. "Is Agnes here?"

Douglas shook his head. "Not coming because of the baby. Once he's on a better schedule I'm sure she'll be here."

I mingled with the crowd, glad to see Byron and Marguerite, our grand masters, talking together. Trays of food had been brought out and placed on a long oak table next to several open bottles of champagne. Becky arrived by my side and handed me a glass full of the bubbling liquid. "This is in celebration for new beginnings," she said, taking a sip. She hadn't braided her hair and it hung around her shoulders, a nimbus of bright color.

I fiddled with my unruly tangle that had grown down past my shoulders. I hadn't spent much time getting ready, imagining a night in darkness. I clinked my glass with hers. "To new beginnings." I took a sip and nearly sneezed from the bubbles. "When will we go outside?"

"Soon, I expect. We're lucky it's a clear night. The moon should be up any minute now."

Twenty minutes later the lights in the ballroom were extinguished, signaling that it was time to head outside. We assembled in a circle on the spacious patio, waiting for Byron and Marguerite to begin the ritual. The two grand masters moved to the center of the circle, their faces pale in the light of the moon as they lifted them. Marguerite was wearing a deep blue robe, Byron in forest green. Although these two were not married I had the feeling that they loved each other, and spent many a night in the same bed.

"We call all the spirits of this full moon night to come to our aid. There are many among us who have questions or who need guidance tonight. Oh goddess moon we feel your magic, we bow to you and take in your power to use only for good!"" They moved together to kiss briefly before filling the small bowls with rosewater. They walked in different directions around the circle sprinkling the water among the crowd before meeting on the other side.

They bowed to each other before moving to the middle of the circle. "We call upon your wisdom!" they cried, looking upward at the bright orb. "All those in need step forward now!"

I watched others step into the center, surprised when I felt a push from behind that propelled me forward. I turned, but saw no one behind me.

"Those who have questions, send your prayers upward. Listen closely for the answers." They chanted quietly while all of us stared upward. "Please, Aine, I need your wisdom and your strength to see my way forward. I love Jerry, but I'm afraid I've hurt him too deeply. Will he return? Can I give up my stubborn and controlling ways to let him into my heart? And can he give me what I need?" I stood there, listening to the whisper of wind in the tall conifers behind the patio. "You must have faith," came down to me, as though tiny wings had flown by my ears. When tears came I let them fall.

A few moments later Byron moved into the circle, his gestures moving us all back. "We give thanks for your wisdom, goddess moon." He bowed low, all of us doing the same, our hands in prayer position. He and Marguerite chanted for another few minutes before his loud voice declared it too cold. There was a titter of laughter and then we all filed back inside.

The scene inside was giddy. The rest of the champagne was consumed, people talking and laughing as they met with their friends. When the crowd finally dispersed I followed Valerie and Becky toward the car. "Did you push me into the circle?" I asked Becky once we were inside the car.

"No. I was in the circle with you."

When I glanced toward her mother, Valerie said, "And I wasn't anywhere near you."

"Well, then who was it?"

Becky turned in her seat, her eyebrows rising. "Maybe it was your ghost."

For some reason that explanation did not seem too far-fetched.

CHAPTER TWENTY-FIVE

I ignored Christmas, but spent New Year's Eve with Becky and Valerie, the three of us cooking a turkey and all the trimmings in the apartment above Tarot and Tea. I'd finally remembered to give Becky the Clan Henderson coat-of-arms I'd bought in Scotland.

She examined it and handed it to Valerie. "I'm going to have it framed and hang it in the bakery."

"This is just perfect," Valerie said, gazing at the two of us as we toasted the New Year with the champagne I'd purchased.

But I wasn't feeling the perfection, my mind going to Jerry and Agnes and the fact that I hadn't heard from either one of them.

After our meal, and while we were cleaning up, I asked Valerie again about reading the Tarot cards for my clients. "I've been trying to come up with ways to bring in more money. Mom named it Tarot and Tea for a reason. I'll pay you a weekly salary if you like."

Valerie laughed. "You don't have to pay me. After all your help with Becky, I owe you. And besides, I don't need the money. We can try it and see if it works out. I do like your clientele, and the shop's energy feels good to me."

"Great! I'll put an advertisement in the local paper." We settled on a start date and made a loose plan for what days and possible times.

Later I refused Valerie's offer of a ride home, telling her I wanted to be out in the cold with my thoughts and plans for the New Year. I walked through the cold streets, my hands stuck deep in my pockets, surprised when I saw the flashing lights from the police cruiser behind me. My heart raced. Jerry.

"Are you nuts?" Sam said pulling up beside me. "It's freezing! Get in. I'll give you a ride home."

I climbed in trying to hide my disappointment. "How's things?" I asked.

"I'm back at work. I pulled the graveyard shift tonight, and Agnes isn't happy about it." He chuckled. "She got used to the help." He turned to me. "You need to give her a call, Summer. She thinks you're mad at her. She misses you."

"She does? I thought she was mad at *me*."

He scoffed. "She tends to get caught up in melodrama, and the thing between you and Jerry made her feel like she had to take sides. Have you heard from him?"

I shook my head and stared out the windshield, watching the houses drift by in the dark as we passed. There were no lights on anywhere. Ames wasn't a partying town.

"He's been going through some major changes. I've never seen this side of him. I could tell you some things, but I think he'd be pissed if I did."

"What kind of changes? Is he living with his mother again, or has he found a new girlfriend?"

Sam laughed. "You aren't even close. No new girlfriend, and as far as his mother's concerned, I think he's finally cut the apron strings—hers, that is."

We pulled up in front of my cottage. "Thanks for the ride, Sam. Tell Agnes I still love her."

He smiled. "I will. And don't be surprised if Jerry suddenly appears on your doorstep."

"I wish he would. I've kind of given up on him."

"Don't do that," he said with a wink.

I climbed out and slammed the door closed, waving before hurrying into the cottage.

On the fifth of January Becky rushed into Tarot and Tea from upstairs, her eyes bright with happiness. "They found it, Summer! They found all my stuff!"

"I'm so happy for you!"

"Jerry is a miracle worker! Mom's giving me a ride to the station now, to thank him personally."

I didn't say anything, turning away to hide the tears that welled.

"I'm sorry. I didn't mean to—"

I waved away her apology. "I'm fine. I just need to stop expecting something that's never going to happen."

"Have faith," she said, echoing the words I'd heard on coven night. She hurried toward the door.

After she'd gone Mrs. Browning came up to me, her birdlike gaze as savvy as ever. "That nice policeman is thinking about you," she said.

"Don't say that," I snapped. "I haven't heard from him in a month and a half."

She smiled and walked away. When she came up later with a small bottle of lavender oil, I tried not to meet her gaze, ringing her up silently.

"You will need all your wits when he comes around again," Mrs. Browning said before heading toward the door.

Okay—what did that mean?

I shook my head and tried to get his image out of my mind. The man was as bad as a ghost now, the way he haunted me.

At a little after two in the afternoon the Honda people called to say they'd completed my car. "But I never heard back. Are you letting me pay over time?"

"Didn't you get our text? You can pay in four increments."

"How much is the bill?"

"Twelve-hundred."

"I could have bought another car for that."

"Not as good as this one. She's practically brand new now."

"I don't have a way to get there."

"We can send a car—where do you live?"

I organized for them to send the car to Tarot and Tea at five o'clock, a half an hour before they closed.

I drove my 'practically brand new' car home, glad of the purring sound the engine made and the way she jumped to attention when I put my foot down on the gas. She did seem better. When I parked I heard Cutty barking. I hurried to the door, hoping he hadn't gotten locked in again. But the only thing he seemed was happy to see me. "What's with you?" I asked picking him up. He licked my face.

I was inside when my phone rang. Agnes. "Hi, I was just about to call you," I said, which was true.

"I'm so sorry," she said. "I think the birth hormones made me crazy. I'm better now, but good grief, one minute I was angry, the next crying, and the minute after that I was utterly depressed!"

"I've heard that having a baby can do that."

Agnes cooed to the baby. "You need one of these," she said. "He is such a delight! Although I'm a bit overwhelmed without Sam to help."

"I would need a man in my life in order for that to happen."

Agnes laughed. "What, no immaculate conception for you? Seriously, Summer, haven't you heard from Jerry yet?"

"Not yet. What have you heard?"

There was a long silence. "I've heard a lot—in fact my ears are burning— but I'm bound to secrecy."

"I wish I'd hear something."

"Any more from your ghost?"

"Which one? Finlay or Owen?"

"I was thinking Owen, but either, I suppose."

"Finlay is no longer in the graveyard, and as to Owen—I let go of him completely on the night of winter solstice."

"I'm glad to hear that. Hanging on to someone who's dead doesn't seem very healthy."

"I can barely remember him now."

"I want you to come over soon. You have to see Sammie! He's so cute! It will make you want one for sure."

"Quit saying that!"

Agnes giggled when the baby let out a happy chortle. "When can you come for dinner?"

"I'm not exactly a social butterfly right now. Anytime you can manage it. I have my car back finally."

"I didn't know it was gone."

I chuckled. "Another important thing I was keeping from you."

"Come for dinner on Friday, okay? I have to go now, Sammie's hungry. Again."

I glanced toward the box tied up with ribbon sitting on the table against the wall—the scarf I'd bought for Agnes and never given her. "There isn't a possibility that you're spoiling him, is there?"

Agnes laughed just before the call ended.

CHAPTER TWENTY-SIX

I had changed into pj's and was sitting in the living room watching the fire when I heard a knock on my door. I peeked out the window, very surprised to see Jerry on my stoop. I opened the door. "You're the last person I expected to see."

He watched me solemnly. "Can I come in?"

I opened the door wide and closed it after him. He took off his coat and slung it haphazardly across a chair. "Do you have a beer handy?"

I headed into the kitchen, trying to run my fingers through my tangled hair. I had no make-up on, and the baggy pj's were faded and old. Why hadn't he called ahead? I pulled out a beer and the bottle of wine, pouring myself a glass before joining him on the couch in front of the fire.

I tucked my feet up under me, trying to hide my unshaven legs. "What's happening?"

"I've...I...I've worked some stuff out."

I took a sip and tried to stop the fluttering in my stomach. "You came by at nine o'clock at night to tell me this...without calling ahead?"

"I was on my way home from The Keg and somehow I ended up here."

"Hmm…magic at work?"

"Listen, Summer, I know it's been a long time. I've done a lot of thinking."

He looked older, more serious, his hair longer. He'd begun to grow a beard by the look of things. "And this thinking…was it about us?"

He scoffed. "You've been on my mind every day since the last time I saw you."

Okay—that was a surprise. "And?"

"And I've seen a therapist a few times to sort things out."

He had? Jerry couldn't stand therapists. The time he'd been forced by the department to see one he'd been dragged there kicking and screaming. "What did she say?"

"*He* said that I needed to sort out a few things before I could move forward."

The silenced dragged on, Jerry's dark gaze on the flames. "And what were these things?" I finally prompted.

"My relationship with my mother and my family. My relationship with you, and your relationship with Owen."

He looked up, his gaze meeting mine. Was that fear I saw? I was trembling now, sure his next words would be, 'and I'm breaking up with you.' "Did you tell him Owen was a ghost?"

He scoffed. "No, Summer. But I did tell him you loved the guy. He asked me if you were still with him, and I told him no. He also asked me how I felt about you after all of that."

"And what did you say?"

"I told him I loved you." He looked away again. "He talked about my dad's suicide and how I'd buried my feelings about it. He thinks I've been haunted by the scandal around Dad's removal from the force—that I was afraid of what people thought of me because of Dad being a dirty cop. He had me do some rituals around how I talk to myself—the things I say that aren't positive." He gave a short laugh. "It's been hard work and very painful."

My stomach clenched. "I would imagine so, knowing you." I waited for an interminable amount of time for Jerry to continue, but his eyes remained riveted on the fire.

Finally he continued. "The breakdown I had after that case we worked on together, the one where you almost died—the therapist thinks that was directly related to my insecurity."

"Yes, well, that makes sense. But it was you who saved me."

He looked up. "According to him I didn't give myself much credit for that. And it was you who solved the case."

"Jerry, you've saved my life so many times."

He nodded and went on. "We talked a long time about Mom and how to deal with her neediness. I've already confronted her. She isn't happy, but I think she took it in." He gazed at me. "I told her to stay out of my life."

"You mentioned that on the phone when I was in Scotland."

He let out a sigh and turned toward the fire again. "Sam says the guys at the station would do anything for me."

"That doesn't surprise me. You're a good cop, and fair."

He glanced at me. "Sam's been a major support."

"I'm glad—you needed it. I'm so sorry you've had to go through this. I had no idea, since you always have that cocky cop attitude." I laughed. "It kind of turns me on."

His eyes met mine. "It does? According to the therapist, it's a way to hide how insecure I am."

"Don't change your entire personality because of the therapist, Jerry. I like you the way you are."

He smiled for a moment before turning serious again. "He seems to think I've been using excuses to keep us apart. He said that feeling bad about myself, and flying off the handle over nothing, is intimately connected, and has led to our break-ups. Believing my mom over you is a good example."

"But you figured it out."

"Not before accusing you of shit and having you go off to Scotland mad at me. No wonder you had the affair."

"That wasn't why I..."

He ignored me and went on. "He wanted to know if the affair was something I couldn't forgive. I told him I wasn't sure, but I was leaning toward no. He also asked if you loved me. Do you?" When his gaze met mine his eyes had filled with tears.

"Yes, Jerry. I love you."

He sighed and looked down at the floor. "The therapist told me to follow my heart and not to let a past incident keep me from what I wanted, but—"

"But you're breaking up with me."

He frowned and wiped his eyes with the back of his sleeve. "Why would you say that?"

"If you aren't breaking up with me then why are you explaining all this?"

"I thought you'd want to know my process—how I came to be here tonight." He took hold of my hand, cupping it between his. "What I've been trying to say, what I've wanted to say for a very long time, is—" His liquid eyes met mine. "Summer McCloud, will you marry me?"

Fin

A NOTE FROM THE AUTHOR

Sign-up here for my e-mail list to get promos and news about upcoming books!
http://eepurl.com/cyxEBn

If you enjoyed this book please leave a review on Amazon. Just click on title and follow to reviews! (one or two lines only)
To visit my website: http://www.nikkibroadwell.com